Yury Olesha
ENVY

Translated by T. S. Berczynski

ARDIS

Yury Olesha
ENVY

English translation
by T. S. Berczynski

CONTENTS

INTRODUCTION

Yury Olesha's short novel *Envy* was first published in 1927, in *Red Virgin Soil,* a journal edited by Alexander Voronsky. Until the appearance of *Envy,* Olesha, who was born in Elizavetgrad in 1899 and raised in Odessa, was almost completely unknown as a writer. In the beginning of NEP he moved to Moscow where he began working for *Gudok (The Whistle),* a railroad workers' newspaper, in which he published agitational verse under the pseudonym "Zubilo" ("Point Tool"). In the years following the publication of *Envy,* which was an immediate success, until the establishment of the Union of Soviet Writers in 1932, Olesha published the majority of his fiction, including a satirical novel for "children," *Three Fat Men* (1928), which he had written in 1924; two collections of short stories, *Love* (1929) and *The Cherry Stone* (1930); and the play, *A List of Blessings* (1931).

In his speech at the first All-Union Congress of the Union of Soviet Writers, Olesha, in the face of the demand for "socialist realism," defended his earlier work and dedicated himself to the theme of youth, promising "plays and stories" in which the characters would "decide problems of a moral nature." Yet, Olesha provided only one such work with this theme, a scenario entitled *A Strict Youth* (1934). After two editions of selected works already published by Olesha earlier appeared in 1935 and 1936, Olesha published very little fiction. In the late thirties Olesha devoted his attention primarily to film scripts and newspaper reporting and during World War II turned to translation of Turkmenian and Ukrainian writers while he lived in Ashkhabad. During the "thaw" in 1956, after being almost silent for nearly twenty years, most of Olesha's early works were reissued in a collection, and he contributed selections of his notebooks to *Literary Moscow II,* perhaps the most significant publishing event of the "Year of Protest." The final years of his life, until his death in 1960, were devoted to his autobiography, *Not a Day without a Line* (1965), and a screen adaptation of Dostoevsky's *Idiot.*

Envy is Olesha's best work. Stylistically, it represents one of

INTRODUCTION

the most provocative pieces of prose fiction from the 1920's. The problem of style in the novel is complicated by the shift in point of view from first person in Part I to third person in Part II. While Kavalerov's monologue monopolizes Part I and represents the dominant style in the novel, stylistic unity is not sacrificed for the sake of the narrational scheme. In Part II Ivan Babichev's voice dominates, with the aid of a third-person narrator, echoing many of the peculiarities of Kavalerov's heavily poetic language. To speak of Kavalerov's style is in essence to speak of Olesha's style in *Envy*. At the All-Union Congress of Writers in 1934, Olesha admitted that "Kavalerov looked at the world" with his eyes and that the "hues, colors, images, comparisons, metaphors and conclusions of Kavalerov" were his own. Kavalerov's mode embraces the whole work, its conception and realization. He is as much *Envy* for us as he is the "envier" for Ivan Babichev.

Structurally, the text displays a marked disdain for genre lines. Although most commentators refer to this short prose piece as a novel, it is that only in the loosest sense. *Envy* accomodates a variety of materials and means: verse, letters, bureaucratic memoranda, an excerpt from a pamphlet and even a sign. Other devices which distinguish the work from a long, sustained, prose narrative are the shift in point of view already mentioned, the shift to direct dramatic form during Ivan's interrogation and the inclusion of "The Tale of the Meeting of Two Brothers," which serves as a play within the play.

Thematically, *Envy* exhibits a conflict of diametrically opposed views. Kavalerov, who embodies the present, who can be nothing but what he is, is caught in the clash between the brothers Babichev. Andrei, the corpulent Soviet bureacrat, who takes credit for creations not his own, looks to the future through the young, virile soccer player, Volodya Makarov, whom he adopts as a son and who envies the machine and wants to achieve physical perfection. Ivan, a "great impostor," values fantasy above all and claims to have invented "Ophelia," a machine with the aid of which he threatens to reclaim the world for human feelings and hopes to achieve emotional freedom. As Andrei claims Valya, Ivan's daughter, through her involvement with Volodya, Ivan attempts to win back his daughter to the "conspiracy of human feelings" which he has planned and in which he has involved Kavalerov, who is himself in love with Valya. These complex interrelationships and the attendant imagery suggest a variety of possibilities, including both the psychology of Freud and the philosophy of Dostoevsky's *Notes from the Underground.* The rich verbal texture, the concern with perception and the numerous literary allusions reflect the problems of the creative personality in an unreceptive society. Olesha unashamedly examines the relationship between art and life.

Olesha's *Envy* is not easily rendered into English, as previous efforts by other translators have demonstrated; either the sense or the poetry (or sometimes both) of Olesha's prose is sacrificed. This translation is an attempt to be true to the original, as much as possible, to keep both image and idea in tact and to try to transmit some sense of the poetic prose. For this reason, certain liberties have been taken, at times, with what is normally considered "good English usage."

Salem, Oregon   *T. S. Berczynski*

OLESHA // ENVY

I

In the morning he sings in the john. You can imagine what an effervescent and physically-fit person this is. The desire to sing arises in him like a reflex. These songs of his, in which there's neither melody nor words but just a "ta-ra-ra," which he pipes out in permutations, can be interpreted like this:

"How I like to live... ta-ra! ta-ra!.. My bowels are buoyant... ra-ta-ta-ta-ra-ree... In me the fluids flow flawlessly... ra-ta-ta-doo-ta-ta... Gush, guts, gush... tram-ba-ba-boom!"

When he passes by me in the morning on his way from the bedroom (I pretend to be asleep) to the door leading into the viscera of the apartment, the bathroom, my imagination follows him. I hear the commotion in the phone booth of a bathroom, where it's tight for his bulky body. His back bangs against the inner side of the closed door and his elbows hit the walls; he shuffles his feet. Inset in the bathroom door is frosted, oval glass. He turns the switch; the oval is illuminated from within and becomes a beautiful opal-colored egg. With a mental stare I see this egg hanging in the darkness of the corridor.

He weighs about 220 pounds. Not long ago, when walking down stairs somewhere, he noticed how his breasts bounced in beat with his feet. Therefore he decided to add a new series of gymnastic exercises.

This is a model, masculine specimen.

Usually he indulges in gymnastics, not in his own bedroom,

[3]

but in that room of unprescribed purpose where I am kept. Here it's roomier, airier; there's more light, more radiance. In through the open balcony door pours coolness. Besides this, here there's a sink. The mat is moved in from the bedroom. He's stripped to the waist, wearing knit longies fastened by a single button in the middle of his belly. The azure and rose-colored world of the room revolves in the mother-of-pearl objective of the button. When he lays his back on the mat and begins to raise his legs in turn, the button can't bear it. The groin is unveiled. His groin is grand. The tender spot. The forbidden corner. The groin of a production man. It's the same such groin of suede dullness I saw on a buck antelope. The girls, his secretaries and clerks, would certainly be penetrated by love currents from just one glimpse of it.

He washes like a little boy: pipes, hops, snorts, emits howls. He captures water by handfuls and not quite getting it to his armpits, splashes the mat. The water scatters on the straw in full, clean drops. The foam falling into the basin bubbles like a pancake. Sometimes the soap blinds him—swearing, he tears at his eyelids with his thumbs. He rinses his throat with a screech. Under the balcony people stop and throw back their heads.

The rosiest, quietest morning. Spring in full swing. On all the window sills stand flower boxes. Through their slits seeps the cinnabar of a forthcoming florescence.

(Things don't like me. Furniture tries to trip me. Once some sort of lacquered corner literally bit me. With my blanket I always have complex interrelations. Soup which is served me never cools. If some kind of trinket—a coin or a cuff link—falls off the table, it usually rolls under some piece of almost immovable furniture. I crawl along the floor and, raising my head, I see how the sideboard is laughing.)

The blue straps of his suspenders hang at his sides. He goes to the bedroom, finds his pince-nez on the table, puts it on in front of the mirror and returns to my room. Here, standing in the center, he raises the straps of his suspenders, both at once, with such a movement as if hoisting a load onto his shoulders. He doesn't say a word to me. I pretend to be asleep. In the metallic plates of his suspenders the sun concentrates in two burning bundles. (Things like him.)

[4]

He doesn't have to comb his hair or groom his beard and mustache. His hair is cut short; his mustache is short—just under the nose. He resembles a grown-up fat boy.

He took a bottle; the glass stopper squeaked. He poured Eau du Cologne into his palm and passed the palm along the sphere of his head from his forehead to the nape of his neck and back again.

In the morning he drinks two glasses of cold milk: he gets the pitcher from the sideboard, pours and drinks without sitting down.

My first impression of him stunned me. I can't have assumed or supposed it. Smelling of Eau de Cologne, he stood before me in an elegant gray suit. His lips were fresh, slightly protruded. It turned out he's a dude.

At night I'm often awakened by his snoring. In a daze, I don't understand what's the matter. It's as if someone utters threateningly over and over: "Krakatou... Krra... ka... touuu..."

They've given him a magnificent apartment. You should see the vase that stands on a lacquered pedestal near the balcony door. A vase of the thinnest china, round, tall, transilluminated with a delicate blood-vessel redness. It resembles a flamingo. The apartment is on the third floor. The balcony hangs out in the open. The wide suburban street looks like a highway. Across the street below there's a garden: a thick tree-ridden garden, typical of Moscow suburbs, an unarranged assemblage which grew up on an empty lot walled-in on three sides, like an oven.

He's a glutton. He has dinner out. Last night he came home hungry and decided to have a snack. There was nothing in the sideboard. He went downstairs (there's a store on the corner) and hauled back a whole bunch of stuff: half a pound of ham, a can of sprats, canned mackerel, a large loaf of bread, a good-sized half-moon of Dutch cheese, four apples, ten eggs and "Persian Pea" candied fruits. Fried eggs and tea were ordered (there's a communal kitchen in the house where two cooks take turns serving).

"Dig in, Kavalerov," he invited me and bore down himself. He ate the fried eggs right from the pan and removed the bits of shell as if he were chipping off enamel. His eyes became bloodshot; he took off and put on his pince-nez, smacked his lips, snorted; and his ears moved.

OLESHA

I amuse myself with observations. Have you ever noticed how salt falls off the end of a knife without leaving a trace—the knife shines as if it were never touched; that a pince-nez runs over the bridge of a nose like a bicycle; that a person is surrounded by little inscriptions, a sprawling anthill of small inscriptions: on forks, spoons, plates, the rim of a pince-nez, buttons, pencils? No one notices them. They struggle for existence. They pass from one form to another, up to immense sign-board letters! They rise up—class against class: the letters of street signs wage war with the letters of playbills.

He ate his fill. He reached for the apples with a knife but only slit the yellow cheek of an apple and discarded it.

One people's commissar praised him highly in a speech:

"Andrei Babichev is one of the state's most remarkable people."

He, Andrei Petrovich Babichev, occupies the post of director of the food industry trust. He's a mighty sausage maker, confectioner, and cook.

And I, Nikolai Kavalerov, am a jester in his presence.

II

He heads everything that concerns glutting.

He's greedy and jealous. He'd like to fry all the eggs, pies, cutlets and to bake all the bread himself. He'd like to give birth to food. He gave birth to "Two Bits."

His offspring is growing. "Two Bits" will be a giant institution, the largest cafeteria, the largest kitchen. A two-course dinner will cost two bits.

War is declared on kitchens.

A thousand kitchens can be considered captured.

He'll put an end to homemade, the half-cup and the pint bottle. He'll amalgamate all the meat grinders, hot plates, fry pans, faucets... If you please, this will be the industrialization of kitchens.

He organized a number of committees. The Soviet-built machines

[6]

for cleaning vegetables turned out perfect. A German engineer is building the kitchen. Many factories are fulfilling Babichev's orders.

I found out this about him.

He, director of a trust, with briefcase under arm one morning —a citizen of very solid, obviously state material—ascended an unfamiliar staircase among the charms of a service entrance and knocked on the first door he came to. Like some Harun al-Rashid he visited one of the kitchens in a surburban, proletarian residence. He saw the soot and filth, frantic furies were flitting in the smoke and children were crying. He attacked everything at once. He disturbed everyone—immense, cutting off much of their space, light, and air. Besides this, he had his brief case, wore his pince-nez and was elegant and clean. And the furies decided: this is certainly a member of some committee. Hands on hips, the housewives laid into him. He left. Because of him (they shouted after him) the hot plate went out, a glass broke, and the soup was oversalted. He left without saying what he'd come to say. He has no imagination. He should have said it like this:

"Women! We will blow the soot off you, clean your nostrils of smoke, your ears of din. We'll make a potato magically throw off its own peel in a split second. We'll return to you the hours stolen from you by the kitchen—you'll get half your life back. You, young wife, cook soup for your husband. And you give half your day to a peewee puddle of soup. We'll turn your peewee puddles into shining seas. We'll ladle out cabbage soup by the ocean, pour out buckwheat by the burial mound, gelatin will move by the glacier! Listen, housewives, wait! We promise you: a tile floor will be bathed in sunshine, bronze vats will gleam, plates will be lily white clean, milk will be thick like mercury, and such a fragrance will float from the soup, that the flowers on the table will be envious."

Like a fakir he's in ten places at the same time.

In interoffice memos he often resorts to parenthesis and underscoring; he's afraid that they won't understand and that they'll get something wrong.

Here are samples of his memos:

To Comrade Prokudin!
Make the candy wrappers (12 samples) in compliance

[7]

with the consumer (chocolate, bonbons) but in a novel way. But no "Rosa Luxemburg" (I found out there already is one like that, a fruit paste). Better stick to something from science (poetic—geography? astronomy?), with a name that's serious and irresistible in sound: "Eskimo?" "Telescope?" Call me at the office tomorrow, Wednesday, between one and two. Without fail.

To Comrade Fominsky!

Have them put a piece of meat (cut accurately, *as in a private restaurant*) on every first-course plate (of both the fifty and seventy-five *kopeck dinners).* Make sure this is done. Is it true that: 1) the beer snacks are served without a tray? 2) the peas are small and insufficiently soaked?

He's small-minded, distrustful and as tedious as a housekeeper. At ten o'clock in the morning he arrived from the cardboard factory. Eight people were waiting to be received. He received: 1) the superintendent of the curing plant, 2) the representative of the far-eastern canning trust (he grabbed a can of crabs and ran out of the office to show someone; having returned he put it right next to his elbow and for the longest time couldn't relax; he constantly looked at the light blue can, laughed and scratched his nose), 3) an engineer from the warehouse construction site, 4) a German—concerning trucks (they spoke German; he must have ended the conversation with a proverb because it came out in a rhyme and they both burst out laughing), 5) an artist who brought a design for an advertising poster (he didn't like it; he said that the blue should be obscure—chemical—and not romantic), 6) some contractor-restaurant manager with cuff-links in the shape of milk-white jingles, 7) a seedy man with a curly beard who spoke about heads of cattle, and finally, 8) some delightful village inhabitant. This last meeting was of a special nature. Babichev stood up and moved forward, almost opening wide an embrace. The other filled up the whole office—so captivatingly clumsy, shy, smiling, suntanned, bright-eyed, like that Levin out of Tolstoy. He smelled of field flowers and dairy products. They talked about the state farms. A dreamy expression appeared on the faces of those present.

At four-twenty he went to a conference at the Supreme Soviet of National Economy.

III

In the evening he sits at home blanketed by the palm tree green of a lamp shade. Before him are sheets of paper, notebooks, and little slips with columns of figures. He throws back pages of the desk calendar, jumps up, checks the book rack, takes out some packets, and with his belly on the table, supporting his fat face with his hands, reads. The green field of the table is covered with a sheet of glass. So what is so special about that? A man is working, a man is at home in the evening working. A man staring at a piece of paper is twisting a pencil in his ear. Nothing special. But his whole behavior says: you are a Philistine, Kavalerov. Of course, he doesn't state this. There musn't even be anything of the sort on his mind. But it's clear without words. Some third person announces it to me. Some third person forces me to fly into a fit at the very time I'm watching him.

"Two Bits! Two Bits Esquire!" he shouts. "Two Bits Esquire!"

He suddenly begins to guffaw. He's read something hilarious on one of the papers or seen it in a column of figures. Choking with laughter he beckons me. He snorts and pokes his finger at a sheet of paper. I look and don't see anything. What tickled him? There, where I can't even make out bases for comparison, he sees something deviating so from these bases that he's collapsing with laughter. I heed him with horror. This is the laughter of a fanatic. I listen to him as a blind man listens to the explosion of a skyrocket.

"You are a Philistine, Kavalerov. You don't understand anything."

He doesn't say this but it's clear without words.

Sometimes he doesn't return home until late at night. Then I receive my instructions over the phone:

"Is this Kavalerov? Listen, Kavalerov! They'll be calling me from Bread Supply. Have them call two—seventy-three—zero five. Extension sixty-two. Write it down. Have it? Extension sixty-two, Head of Concessions. So long."

Actually, they do call from Bread Supply.

I ask them to repeat.

"Bread Supply? Comrade Babichev is at Head of Concessions...
What? At Head of Concessions, two—seventy-three—zero five, extension
sixty-two, write it down. Have it? Extension sixty-two, Head of Concessions. So long."

Bread Supply calls trust director Babichev. Babichev is at Head
of Concessions. What do I have to do with this? But I feel good for
having participated indirectly in the fate of Bread Supply and Babichev. I experience administrative ecstasy. But my part is really insignificant. The pawn's part. What can it be? Do I respect him? Fear
him? No. I think I'm just as good as he is. I'm not a Philistine. I'll
prove it.

I'd like to catch him at something, uncover his weak side, an
unprotected point. When I first happened to see him getting dressed
in the morning I was sure that I'd caught him, that I'd broken his im-
penetrability.

Drying himself, he walked from his room to the balcony doorway
and, twisting the towel in his ears, turned his back to me. I saw this
back, the tubby torso, from behind, in the sunlight, and almost scream-
ed. His back gave away everything. His body oil yellowed tenderly. The
scroll of another fate unrolled before me. Babichev's ancestors had
pampered their skin; rolls of fat were gently arranged along the backs
of his ancestors. As an inheritance to the commissar was passed on the
delicateness of skin, the noble color and the pure pigmentation. But
the main thing, that which filled me with a sense of victory, was that
on the small of his back I saw a birthmark, a special hereditary, aris-
tocratic birthmark—that very blood-filled, translucent, tender little
thing, standing out from the body on a small stem, by which after dec-
ades mothers recognize their kidnapped children.

"You are a lord, Andrei Petrovich! You're pretending!" almost
popped out of my mouth.

But he turned his chest toward me.

On his chest, under the right collarbone, was a scar. Round
and puffed out like the imprint of a coin on wax. As if a branch had
grown in that spot and had been chopped off. Babichev was in a work

camp. He was escaping and they shot him.

"Who is Jocasta?" he asked me once out of the blue. Out of him pop questions most unusual in their unexpectedness (especially in the evening). He's busy all day. But his eyes glide along the playbills, the store windows; but the edges of his ears catch words from the conversations of others. He's charged with raw material. I'm his only non-business interlocutor. He senses the need to start a conversation. He considers me incapable of a serious conversation. He's aware that when people are relaxing they chat. He decides to make some sort of contribution to the universal habits. Then he asks me idle questions. I answer them. I'm a fool in his presence. He thinks that I'm a fool.

"Do you like olives?" he asks.

"Yes, I know who Jocasta is! Yes, I like olives, but I don't want to answer stupid questions. I don't think I'm any more stupid than you are." That's how I should answer him. But I don't have enough courage. He crushes me.

IV

I've been living under his roof for two weeks. Two weeks ago he picked me up, drunk, at night near the doorway of a beer hall...

They'd kicked me out of the beer hall. The argument in the beer hall gained momentum gradually; at first nothing even hinted at a scandal—on the contrary, a friendship could have sprung up between the two tables; drunks are sociable; that big group, where the woman was sitting, suggested I join them, and I was prepared to accept the invitation, but the woman, who was charming, slender, in a blue blouse hung loosely on her collar bones, cracked a joke at my expense, and I was insulted and, reversing course in mid-stream, returned to my table carrying my mug before me like a lantern.

Then a whole deluge of jokes poured down after me. I might even have really seemed funny: such a shaggy fellow. In pursuit a man roared in a bass. They threw peas. I walked around my table and stood facing them—beer splattered on the marble, I couldn't free my thumb which was entangled in the handle of the mug—half looped, I burst with confession; self-abasement and insolence merged into one bitter torrent:

"You... are a troop of monsters... a wandering troop of freaks
kidnapping a girl... (The bystanders were listening; the shaggy fellow
expressed himself strongly, his speech came out of the common din.)
You, sitting on the right under the palm, are freak number one. Stand
and show everyone... Take note, comrades, respected public... Quiet!
Orchestra, a waltz! A melodic, neutral waltz! Your face represents a
harness. The cheeks are drawn tight by wrinkles—and these aren't
wrinkles but reins; your chin is an ox, your nose the driver sick with
leprosy, and the rest is the load on the cart... Sit down. Next: monster
number two... The man with cheeks that look like knees... Very pret-
ty! Feast your eyes, citizens, on the troop of freaks passing through...
And you? How did you get in through this door? Didn't your ears
get stuck? And you, clinging to the kidnapped girl, ask her, what does
she think about blackheads? Comrades... (I turned in all directions)
they... these right here... they laughed at me. That one there laughed...
Do you know how you laughed? You emitted the sort of sounds an
empty enema emits... Maiden... 'in gardens crowned by vernal hue,
tsaritsa, no such rose appears, which might attempt a war with you,
with you or with your eighteen years!...' Maiden! Shout! Call for
help! We'll save you. What's happened to the world? He's touching
you and you hesitate? Do you understand? (I made a pause and then
spoke triumphantly.) I'm calling you. Sit here with me. Why did you
laugh at me? I stand before you, a young lady I don't know, and beg:
don't lose me. Simply stand, push them away and step over here. What
do you expect from him, from all of them? What?... Tenderness?
intellect? caresses? faithfulness? Come to me. It's funny for me even
to be competing with them. You'll receive immeasurably more from
me..."

I spoke, horrified by what I was saying. I distinctly remember
those particular dreams in which you know it's a dream and, knowing
you'll wake up, do what you want. But here it was apparent: awakening wouldn't follow. The tangle of irreparability rabidly entwined.

They threw me out.

I was lying unconscious. Then having come to, I said:

"I call them, but they don't come. I call these swine, but they
don't come." (My words referred to all women at once.)

I was lying over a sewer hole with my face on the grating. In the sewer, from which I drew in air, there was rankness, the swarming of rankness; in the black vapor of the sewer something moved, the muck was alive. Falling, I caught sight of the sewer for an instant and the memory of it dominated my dreams. It was the condensation of the anxiety and the fear suffered in the beer hall, the humiliation and the fear of punishment—I was running away, escaping—all my energies strained, and the dream broke.

I opened my eyes trembling with the joy of deliverance. But the awakening was so incomplete that I took it for a transition from one vision to another, and in the new vision the main role was played by my deliverer—the one who saved me from persecution, that someone whose hands and sleeves I showered with kisses, thinking that I was kissing in a dream—whose neck I put my arms around, sobbing bitterly.

"Why am I so miserable?... How hard it is for me to live in this world!" I babbled.

"Put his head higher," said the savior.

They took me in a car. Coming to, I saw the sky, a pale sky becoming brighter; it drifted from my heels to behind my head. This vision thundered, it was dizzying and every time ended with a storm of nausea. When I woke up in the morning, in fear I stretched my arm toward my feet. Having not yet figured out where I was, what was happening to me, I remember jolts and rocking. The thought struck me that they'd taken me in an ambulance, that when I was drunk they'd cut off my legs. I stretched my arms sure that I would find a thick barrel-like roundness of bandage. But it turned out simply: I was lying on a sofa in a large, clean and bright room, which had a balcony and two windows. It was early morning. Turning pink, the stone of the balcony warmed peacefully.

When we got acquainted in the morning, I told him about myself.

"You were a sorry sight," he said, "I felt very sorry for you. Perhaps you take offense: so to say, a man meddles in another's life? Then excuse me, please. But if you want to, now: live normally for a while. I would be very glad. There's a lot of room. Light and air. And there's work for you: there's some proofreading, work-up of materials. Want to?"

What motives compelled this famous personality to condescend so to a strange, suspicious-looking young man?

V

One evening two secrets were revealed.

"Andrei Petrovich," I asked, "who is that, in the frame?"

On his desk stands a photograph of a dark-complexioned youth.

"What's that?" He always requests repetition. His thoughts stick to the paper; he can't tear them off right away. "What's that?" And he's absent still.

"Who's that young man?"

"Ah... That's someone named Volodya Makarov. A remarkable young man." (He never speaks normally with me. As if I couldn't ask him about anything serious. It always seems to me that in answer I receive from him a proverb, or a couplet, or simply mumblings. Like now —instead of answering with the normal modulation, "remarkable young man," he scans, almost as if making a recitation, "mah-nn!")

"What's remarkable about him?" I ask, avenging myself with the bitterness of my tone.

But he doesn't notice any bitterness.

"Nothing really. Simply a young man. A student. You sleep on his sofa," he said. "The thing is that he's sort of my son. He's been living with me for ten years. Volodya Makarov. Right now he's away. At his father's. In Murom."

"Oh, that's how it is..."

"That's it."

He got up from the desk, paced.

"He's eighteen. He's a star soccer player."

(Ah, a soccer player, I thought.)

"Why," I said, "that really is remarkable! To be a star soccer player—that's in truth a great quality." (What am I saying?)

He didn't hear. He's in the power of blissful thoughts. From the balcony doorway he looks into the distance at the sky. He's thinking about Volodya Makarov.

"This youth is not at all like anyone else," he said, suddenly turning toward me. (I see that the fact that I am present here when this same Volodya Makarov is in his thoughts is insulting to him.) "In the first place, I owe him my life. Ten years ago he saved me from the death penalty. They were supposed to put the back of my head down on an anvil and bash my face with a hammer. He saved me. (He likes to talk about that one's feat. Apparently he often recalls the feat.) But that's not important. Something else is important. He's a completely new man. Well, all right." (And he returned to the desk.)

"Why did you pick me up and bring me here?"

"What's that? Huh?" He's mumbling; only in a second will he hear my question. "Why did I bring you here? You were a sorry sight. It was impossible not to be touched. You were sobbing. I felt sorry for you."

"And the sofa?"

"What about the sofa?"

"When your boy returns..."

Without a moment's hesitation he answered simply and gaily:

"Then you'll have to give up the sofa..."

I should get up and hit him in the puss. You see, he took pity, he, an illustrious personality, felt sorry for an unfortunate young man who'd gone astray. But temporarily. Until the star returns. He's simply bored in the evenings. And later on he'll chase me out. He talks about it cynically.

"Andrei Petrovich," I say. "Do you understand what you said? You're a boor!"

"What's that? Huh?" His thoughts tear away from the paper. Right now his hearing will repeat my sentence to him and I implore fate that his hearing makes a mistake. Did he really hear? Well, let him. At once.

But an external circumstance interferes. I'm not yet fated to fly from this house.

Out on the street under the balcony someone shouts:

"Andrei!"

He turns his head.

"Andrei!"

[15]

He gets up abruptly, pushing himself away from the desk with his palm.

"Andrusha! Dear boy!"

He goes out onto the balcony. I go up to the window. We're both looking at the street. Darkness. The pavement is only slightly illuminated by the windows. In the middle stands a short, broad-shouldered man.

"Good evening, Andrusha. How are you? How's 'Two Bits?' "

(From the window I see the balcony and huge Andrusha. He's snorting; I can hear.)

The man on the street continues to exclaim, but a little quieter:

"Why're you silent? I came to give you some news. I've invented a machine. The machine is called 'Ophelia.' "

Babichev quickly turns. His shadow is cast perpendicularly across the street and almost produces a storm in the foliage of the garden on the other side. He sits down at the desk and taps his fingers on the glass.

"Watch out, Andrei!" a shout is heard. "Don't get carried away! I'll ruin you, Andrei ..."

Then Babichev again jumps up and flies out onto the balcony with clenched fists. The trees are definitely raging. His shadow rushes down on the city like Buddha.

"Against whom are you waging war, scoundrel?" he says. Thereupon the railings shake. He pounds with his fist. "Against whom are you waging war, scoundrel? Get out of here. I'll have you arre-e-ested."

"Good-bye," resounds from below.

The chubby man takes off his hat, stretches his arm and waves with his hat (a derby? It seems, a derby?); his politeness is affected. Andrei is no longer on the balcony; quickly sowing his small steps the man moves off down the center of the street.

"There!" Babichev shouts at me. "There, feast your eyes. My little brother Ivan. Such a swine!"

He walks around the room boiling. And once again shouts at me:

"Who's he,—Ivan? Who? A loafer, a harmful, infectious man. He should be shot!"

(The dark-complexioned youth in the portrait is smiling. He has a plebian face. He shows his especially sparkling teeth manfully. He exhibits a whole glittering cage of teeth—like a Japanese.)

VI

Evening. He's working. I'm sitting on the sofa. Between us there's a lamp. The lamp shade (as seen by me) obliterates the upper part of his face; it isn't there. The lower hemisphere of his head hangs under the lamp shade. On the whole it resembles a painted, clay piggy bank.

"My youth coincided with the youth of the century," I say.

He's not listening. His indifference to me is insulting.

"I often think about the century. Our century is famous. And it's a beautiful fate—isn't it?—if they coincide:

His hearing responds to the rhyme. Rhyme—it's funny for a serious man.

"Century-man," he repeats. (But tell him that he had just heard and repeated two words and he wouldn't believe it.)

"In Europe there's plenty of chance for a talented man to achieve glory. There they love another's glory. If you will, just do something remarkable and they'll pick you up under the arms and lead you onto the road to glory... We don't have any means for individual achievement of success. Isn't that so?"

It's the same as if I were talking to myself. I resound, pronounce words—go ahead, resound. Not even my resounding disturbs him.

In our country the roads to glory are obstructed by barriers... A talented man must either abate or dare to raise the barrier with a big scandal. I, for example, would like to argue. I like to show the strength of my personality. I want my own glory. We're afraid to give a man attention. I want more attention. I would like to have been born in a small French town, to have grown up in daydreams, to have set myself some sort of high goal, and one fine day to have walked out of that small town and come to the capital on foot, and

there, working fanatically, to have reached my goal. But I wasn't
born in the West. Now they've told me: it's not that it's yours—even
the most remarkable personality is nothing. And I'm gradually becoming accustomed to this truth, against which it's impossible to argue. I even look at it like this: after all, you can get famous by becoming a musician, a waiter, a military leader, crossing Niagara Falls
on a tightrope... These are the legitimate means of attaining fame;
here the personality tries to show itself... But just imagine, while
from a man is expected a sober, realistic approach to things and
events—suddenly to just pick up and create something obviously ab-
sured, to perpetrate some sort of ingenious prank and then to say:
"So that's the way you are and this is the way I am." To come out
on a square and do whatever you'd like and exit bowing: I lived, I
did what I wanted to do.

He doesn't hear anything.

"If only to pick up and do it like this: to kill yourself. Suicide
without any motive. Out of mischief. To show that everyone has the
right to dispose of himself. Even now. To hang myself at your entrance way."

"Better yet, hang yourself at the entrance way of the VSNH on
Barbarian Square, now Mogin Square. There's a huge arch there. Seen
it? There it would come off effectively."

In the room where I lived before my migration, there stands a
frightful bed. I feared it like a ghost. It's concave just like a keg. Your
bones rattle in it. On it there's a blue blanket purchased by me in
Kharkov at the Annunciation Bazaar in a year of famine. An old woman was selling pies. They were covered with a blanket. Cooling, not
yet having given up the heat of life, they almost muttered under the
blanket, romped like puppies. At that time I lived poorly like everyone else, and this composition breathed with such abundance, home-
likeness and warmth that on that day I made a firm decision: to buy
myself such a blanket. The dream came true. One fine evening I
crawled under the blue blanket. I boiled under it, romped; the
warmth drove me to shaking as if I were gelatinous. This was delightful drowsing. But time went by and the designs on the blanket
swelled and turned into pretzel-shaped biscuits.

Now I sleep on an excellent sofa.

By intentional shaking I excite the ringing of its new, light, virginal springs. There result individual droplets of ringing, running out of the depth. The idea of bubbles of air rising to the surface of water arises. I fall asleep like a child. On the sofa I make a flight to childhood. Bliss attends me. Like a child I'm once again in command of the small time interval which separates the first weight shift of the eyelids, the first bleariness, from the beginning of real sleep. I once again know how to prolong this interval, to savor it, to fill it with my kind of thoughts, and, having not yet plunged into sleep, still having control of my vigilant consciousness—to already see how thoughts acquire dream-world flesh, how bubbles of ringing from submarine depths turn into rapidly spinning grapes, how a succulent bunch of grapes crops up, a whole fence, thickly entangled bunches of grapes; a path along the vineyard, a sunny road, torridity...

I'm twenty-seven years old.

Changing my shirt once, I saw myself in the mirror and suddenly I sort of caught a similarity in me to my father. In reality there is no such similarity. I remembered: my parents' bedroom and I, a small boy, am watching my father changing his shirt. I was sorry for him. It's already too late for him to be handsome, famous; he's already done, finished and nothing more than what he is can he be. That's what I thought, feeling sorry for him and taking pride in my superiority. But now I recognized my father in me. It was a similarity of forms—no, something else: I would say—a sexual similarity: I sort of suddenly sensed my father's seed in me, in my substance. And someone sort of said to me: you're done. Finished. There won't be anything more. Bear a son.

I won't ever be either handsome or famous. I won't come walking from the small town into the capital. I won't be either a military leader or a people's commissar, or a scholar, or an adventurer. I dreamed my whole life of an extraordinary love. Soon I'll return to my old apartment, to the room with the frightful bed. There're dismal surroundings there: the widow Prokopovich. She's about forty-five, but around the house they call her 'Annechka.' She cooks dinner for the barbers' artel. She's set up a kitchen in the corridor. In a dark cavity is a stove. She feeds cats. Silent, slender cats fly up after her hands with electrodynamic movements. She strews some sort of

giblets to them. Because of this the floor is sort of decorated with
mother-of-pearl spit splashes. Once I slipped, having stepped on something's heart—small and tightly formed like a chestnut. She walks enmeshed in cats and the blood vessels of animals. A knife sparkles in her
hand. She tears through intestines with her elbows like a princess
through a cobweb.

The widow Prokopovich is old, fat and flabby. You can squeeze
her out like liver sausage. In the morning I'd catch her at the sink in
the corridor. She'd be undressed and smiling at me with a *feminine*
smile. On a small stool by her door stood a basin and in it floated
combed-out hairs.

The widow Prokopovich is a symbol of my masculine humility.
It comes out like this: please, I'm ready, mistake the door at night, I
purposely won't lock it, I'll take you in. We'll live, enjoy ourselves.
Give up dreams of extraordinary love. Everything's passed. Just look
what's become of you, neighbor: chubby, in pants that don't fit any-
more. Well, what else do you need? That one? The one with slender
hands? The imaginary one? With the egg-shaped face? Forget it.
You're a daddy already. Come on, eh? I have a remarkable bed. The
deceased won it in a lottery. A quilt. I'll look after you. I'll sympa-
thize. Eh?

Sometimes her stare expressed obvious indecency. Sometimes
on meeting me some small sound, a round, vocal drop rolls out of
her throat pushed by a spasm of ecstasy.

I'm no daddy, lousy cook. I'm no dad to you, reptile.

I fall asleep on Babichev's sofa.

I dream that a sweet young thing, laughing lightly, slips toward
me under the sheet. My dreams are coming true. But with what, with
what can I express my gratitude? No one ever loved me without
compensation. And those prostitutes tried to take me for as much
as they could—what will she demand from me? As it should be in a
dream, she guesses my thoughts and says:

"Oh, don't worry. Just two bits."

I remember from years ago: I, a gymnasium student, am taken
to a museum of wax figures. In a glass cube a handsome man in tails,

with a fire-spitting wound in his chest, was dying in someone's arms.

"That's the French president, Carnot, wounded by an anar-
chist," father explained to me.

The president was dying, breathing, the eyelids rolled. Slowly,.
like a clock, went the life of the president. I watched as if spellbound.
A magnificent man, having stuck up his beard, was lying in a greenish
cube. This was magnificent. Then for the first time I heard the rumble
of time. Seasons soared over my head. I swallowed ecstatic tears. I
decided to become famous so that some day my wax double, filled
with the hum of centuries, which only a few are given to hear, would
likewise be posed in a greenish cube.

Now I'm writing a routine for a variety team: monologues and
couplets about tax collectors, sovsocialites, Nepmen and alimonies:

> *In the office noise and tararup,*
> *Long ago things all mixed up:*
> *To typist Lizzy Kaplan from*
> *All of us a new tin drum...*

And still, maybe, someday in a large waxworks exhibition
there will stand a wax figure of a strange man, thicknosed, with a
pale, kind face, with disheveled hair, boyishly plump, in a jacket
which has one button left on the belly; and on the cube there'll be
a plaque:

NIKOLAI KAVALEROV

And nothing more. That's it. And everyone seeing it will say,
"Ah, that's the one who lived at a famous time, hated everyone and
envied everyone, bragged, got carried away, was obsessed with great
plans, wanted to do a lot and did nothing—and ended up by committing a disgusting, malicious crime..."

VII

From Tverskaya Street I turned onto a side street. I had to go to Nikitskaya. Early morning. I move like painful rheumatism from joint to joint. Things don't like me. The side street is down with a case of me.

A little man in a derby was walking in front of me.

At first I thought: he's hurrying—but it soon became apparent that the hurried walk with the heaving of the whole torso was peculiar to the man in general.

He was carrying a pillow. He held suspended by an ear a large pillow in a yellow pillowcase. It bumped against his knee. Because of this cavities appeared and disappeared in it.

It happens that in the center of the city, somewhere on a side street, there'll be set up a romantic, flowering hedge. We were walking along a hedge.

A bird on a branch flashed, twitched and trilled, somehow resembling a machine for clipping hair. The man walking in front glanced back at the bird. Walking behind I managed to catch sight of only the first phase, the half-moon of his face. He was smiling.

"Similar, isn't it?" I nearly exclaimed, sure that the same similarity had come into his head.

The derby.

He takes it off and carries it like a cake, putting his hand around it. In the other hand is the pillow.

The windows are open. In one on the second floor is seen a little blue vase with a flower. The vase attracts the man. He leaves the sidewalk, goes out to the middle of the pavement and stops under the window lifting up his face. His derby slid onto the nape of his neck. He holds the pillow tenaciously. His knee is already flowering with down.

I observe from behind a jut.

He called the vase:

"Valya!"

Instantly in the window, toppling the vase, a girl in something pink wildly appears.

"Valya," he said, "I've come for you."

Silence ensued. Water from the vase ran onto the ledge.

"Look, I brought... See? (He lifted the pillow up in front of his stomach with both hands.) Recognize it? You slept on it. (He laughed.) Come back to me, Valya. Don't you want to? I'll show you 'Ophelia.' Don't you want to?"

Once again silence ensued. The girl was lying face down on the windowsill dangling her disheveled head of hair. Next to her rolled the vase. I remembered that a second after her appearance, the girl, hardly having seen the man standing in the street, had already fallen with her elbows onto the windowsill, and her elbows had collapsed.

Clouds moved across the sky and along the window panes and in the window panes their paths entangled.

"I beg you, Valya, come back! It's simple: run down the stairs."

He waited..

Onlookers stopped.

"Don't you want to? Well, good-bye."

He turned around, adjusted his derby and walked off down the middle of the side street in my direction.

"Wait! Wait, Dad! Dad! Dad!"

He quickened his steps, began running. Past me. I saw that he wasn't young... He choked and turned pale from running. A laughable, plump little man was running with a pillow pressed to his chest. But there was nothing insane in that.

The window emptied.

She plunged into pursuit. She ran up to the corner—there the solitude of the side street ended; she didn't find him. I stood by the hedge. The girl was returning. I stepped toward her. She thought that I could help her, that I knew something, and stopped. A tear, tiring itself out, ran down her cheek as down a vase. She was all elated, ready to ask passionately about something, but I cut her off saying:

"You roared past me like a bough full of flowers and leaves."

In the evening I proofread:

"....Thus, the blood collected during slaughter may be processed either for food, for the preparation of sausage, or for the manufacture of light and dark albumin, glue, buttons, paints, fertilizers and feed for cattle, fowl and fish. The suet of all types of cattle and the fat-retaining organic waste product—for the preparation of edible fats: tallow, margarine, artificial butter, and of industrial oils: stearine, glycerine and lubricative oils. The heads and hooves of sheep with the aid of spiral electric drills, automatic-acting cleaning machines, gas-operated lathes, cutting machines and scalding vats are processed for food products, industrial bone oil, the hair and bones for various articles...."

He's talking on the phone. They call him about ten times a night. There are lots of people he could be talking to. But suddenly reaches me:

"That's not cruelty."

I listen in.

"That's not cruelty. You're asking and I'm telling you. That's not cruelty. No, no! You can be perfectly relaxed. You hear? —Humiliating himself? What? Walks under windows? —Don't believe it. Those are his tricks. He walks under my windows too. He likes to walk under windows. I know him. —What? And? You cried? All evening? You cried all evening for nothing. —He'll go mad? We'll send him to Kanatchikov. Ophelia? Which one? Ah... Spit. Ophelia— that's nonsense. —As you like it. But I say you're doing the right thing. —Yes, yes. —What? A pillow? Really? (Laughter.) I'm imagining. How's that? How's that? The one you slept on? Just think. —What? Every pillow has its history. In short, don't have any doubts. —What? —Yes—yes! (Here he became silent and listened for a long time. I sat on the edge of my seat. He burst out laughing.) A bough? How's that? What kind of bough? Full of flowers? Flowers and leaves? What? That's probably some alcoholic from his crowd."

VIII

Picture to yourself ordinary, cooked, tea-time sausage: a fat, evenly rounded rod cut from the end of a large, ponderous piece. On the blind end, out of the wrinkled skin tied in a knot, dangles a rope tail. Sausage like any other sausage. Its weight is probably a little more than two pounds. The sweaty surface, the yellowing bubbles of subcutaneous fat. At the place where it's cut this same suet has the look of white specks.

Babichev held the sausage in his palm. He was speaking. The doors opened and closed. People came in. Crowded together. The sausage dangled from Babichev's dignified, pink palm like something alive.

"Is that great?" he inquired consulting everyone at once. "No, you take a look... Too bad Shapiro isn't here. We must call Shapiro. Ho-ho. It's great! Have you called Shapiro? Busy? Call again..."

Then the sausage is on the desk. Babichev lovingly arranged its bedding. Moving back and not taking his eyes off it, he himself sat down in an armchair, finding it with his backside, set his fists against his thighs and burst with laughter. He raised a fist, noticed some fat, and licked. "Kavalerov!" (After the laughter.) "Are you free right now? Please go to Shapiro. To the warehouse. You know? Go straight to him and take it. (With eyes on the sausage.) When you bring it, have him look at it and call me."

I brought the sausage to Shapiro at the warehouse. And Babichev phoned all over the place.

"Yes, yes," he roared, "yes! Absolutely the most superior! We'll send it to the exhibition. We'll send it to Milan! The very one! Yes! Yes! Seventy percent veal. A big victory... No, not fifty kopecks, you crank... Fifty kopecks! Ho-ho! For thirty-five. Is that great? A beauty!"

He left.

The laughing face—a rosy, clay pot—swung in the window of the automobile. On his way in he shoved his Tyrolean hat at the doorman and, eyes bulging, ran along the staircase, heavy, noisy and impetuous, like a wild boar. "Sausage!" resounds in many offices. "The very one...I was telling you... A joke!..." From every office, while I was wandering along sun-drenched streets, he called Shapiro:

"They're bringing it to you! Solomon, you'll see! You'll burst..."

"They still haven't brought it? Ho-ho, Solomon..."

He was wiping his sweaty neck, slipping a handkerchief down deep inside his collar almost tearing it, scowling, suffering.

I arrived at Shapiro's. Everyone saw that I was carrying the sausage and everyone made way. The path cleared magically. Everyone knew that a messenger was coming with Babichev's sausage. Shapiro, a melancholic old Jew with a nose which in profile looked like the number six, was standing under a wooden awning in the warehouse courtyard. A door filled with motive summer darkness, like all doors opening onto packing houses (such a gently chaotic darkness arises before your eyes if you close and press your eyelids with your fingers), led into a huge shed. By the door jamb on the outside hung a telephone. Next to it protruded a nail with the yellow sheets of some documents hung on it.

Shapiro took the rod of sausage from me, tested it on the scale, swung it in his palm (simultaneously shaking his head), brought it up to his nose, sniffed. After this, he came out from under the awning, put the sausage on a box and with a penknife carefully cut off a small, soft slice. In complete silence the slice was chewed, pressed to the palate, sucked and slowly swallowed. The hand with the penknife was drawn aside, it was quivering: the hand's owner considered his sensations.

"Ah," he sighed having swallowed. "Babichev's a champ. He's made a sausage. Listen, it's the truth, he's done it. Thirty-five kopecks such sausage—you know; that's quite incredible."

The telephone rang. Shapiro got up slowly and went to the door.

"Yes, Comrade Babichev. I congratulate you and want to kiss you."

From somewhere Babichev was shouting with such force that here, at a considerable distance from the phone, I heard his voice, the crackle and the bursting sounds in the receiver. The receiver, shaking with powerful vibrations, almost tore itself out of Shapiro's weak fingers. He even shook his other hand at it, scowling, as if admonishing a naughty child preventing him from listening.

"What should I do?" I asked. "Will the sausage remain with you?"

"He asks you to bring it home to him, to the apartment. He's inviting me to eat it this evening."

I couldn't restrain myself:

"Do I really have to drag it home? Can't you buy another?"

"To buy such sausage is impossible," mumbled Shapiro. "It

hasn't gone on the market yet. It's a sample from the factory.

"It'll spoil."

Folding the knife and searching for his pocket by sliding his hand along his side, Shapiro pronounced sluggishly, smiling slightly and lowering his eyelids—like old Jews—and preached:

"I congratulated Comrade Babichev on sausage which will not go bad in one day. Otherwise I wouldn't have congratulated Comrade Babichev. We'll eat it up today. Put it in the sun, don't be afraid, in the hot sun—it'll smell like a rose."

He disappeared in the darkness of the shed, returned with wrapping and oil paper, and within a few seconds I was holding a masterfully made packet.

From the first days of my acquaintance with Babichev I had already heard conversations about the famous sausage. Somewhere experiments were proceeding on the preparation of some special sort—nourishing, pure and cheap. Babichev was continually conferring at various places; adopting a faint note of concern, he asked questions and gave advice; sometimes he left the phone languorous, sometimes sweetly excited. Finally the species was derived. Out of the mysterious incubators, rocking with the unwieldy swaying of its trunk, crawled a tightly stuffed intestine.

Having received a section of this intestine Babichev turned red, even felt ashamed at first, like a bridegroom who has noticed how beautiful his young bride is and what an enchanting impression she is making on the guests. In happy confusion he looked around at everyone and instantly put the piece down and pushed it away with such an expression of upraised palms, just as if he wanted to say, "No, no. It's not necessary. I refuse right now so I won't be tormented later. It can't be that such successes have happened in a simple, human life. Here's a trap of fate. Take it away. I'm unworthy."

Carrying two pounds of the wondrous sausage I ambulated in an indefinite direction.

I'm standing on a bridge.

The Palace of Labor is on my left, behind—the Kremlin. On the river are boats, swimmers. A launch slips quickly under my bird's eye view. Instead of a launch, that which I see resembles in form a gigantic, longitudinally sectioned almond. The almond vanishes under the bridge. Only then do I remember the launch's funnel and that near the funnel some two people were eating borshch out of a pot. A white puff of smoke, transparent and disappearing, flies in my direction. It fails to complete its course, changes into other dimensions and reaches me only with its last trace coiling into a barely visible astral hoop.

I wanted to throw the sausage into the river.

A remarkable man, Andrei Babichev, a member of the Society of Political Prisoners, a statesman, considers his day today a holiday. Only because they showed him a new sort of sausage... Is this really a holiday?... Is this really glory?

He beamed today. Yes, the stamp of glory lay on him. Why didn't I feel amorousness, exhilaration, veneration in the sight of this glory? Malice has seized me. He is a statesman, a communist, he's building a new world. And glory flames up in his new world because out of the hands of a sausage maker has come a new sort of sausage. I don't understand this glory; what does it mean? Not of such glory did biographies, monuments, history speak to me... Does it mean that the nature of glory has changed? Everywhere or only here, in the world being built. But I feel that this new world being built is paramount, triumphant... I'm not a blind man, I have a head on my shoulders. It's not necessary to teach me, to explain to me... I'm literate. It's precisely in this world I want glory! I want to beam, as Babichev beamed today. But a new sort of sausage won't make me beam.

I meander along the streets with the package. A piece of lousy sausage directs my movements, my will. I won't have it!

Several times I was ready to fling the package over the railing. But I had only to picture to myself how, freeing itself from the wrapper in flight, the ill-fated piece of sausage falls and with the effect of a torpedo disappears into the waves—when instantly another picture would set me to trembling. Coming down on me I saw Babichev, a thundering, invincible idiot with bulging eyes. I'm afraid of him. He crushes me. He doesn't look at me—but sees right through me. He doesn't look at me. Only from the side do I see his eyes; when his face is turned in my direction his gaze isn't there: only the pince-nez sparkles, two blind, round plates. It's not interesting for him to look at me, no time, no desire, but I understand that he sees right through me.

In the evening Solomon Shapiro came, two more came and Babichev fixed refreshments. The old Jew brought a bottle of vodka and they drank, nibbling on the famous sausage. I refused participation in the repast. I observed them from the balcony.

Painting has immortalized many feasts. Military leaders, doges and simply greasy gluttons are feasting. Epochs are captured. Quill pens wave, fabrics fall, cheeks shine.

New Tiepolo! Hurry here! Here are feasting personages for you... They're sitting around a table under a one-hundred-candle-power lamp, conversing lively. Paint them, new Tiepolo, paint "The Feast at the Industrial Executive's."

I see your canvas in a museum. I see the visitors standing before your picture. They're racking their brains; they don't know what the corpulent giant in blue suspenders, whom you painted, is saying with such inspiration... On a fork he holds a little circle of sausage. The circle should have disappeared into the speaker's mouth long ago, but there's no way it can disappear because the speaker is too carried away with his own speech. What's he talking about?

"Here we don't know how to make sausages!" the giant in the blue suspenders was saying. "Can those be sausages we have? Quiet, Solomon. You're a Jew, you don't understand anything when it comes to sausages—you like cachectic kosher meat... We don't have sausages. These are sclerotic fingers and not sausages. Real sausages should spatter. I'll succeed, you'll see, I'll make such sausages."

IX

We gathered at the air terminal.

I say, "we!" Really, I was just something on the side, a person accidentally attached. No one consulted me; my impressions didn't interest anyone. I could have stayed home with a clear conscience.

The take-off of a newly designed Soviet plane was supposed to take place. They invited Babichev. The guests went out beyond the

barrier. Babichev predominated even in this select society. He had
only to join with someone in conversation when a circle closed
around him. Everyone listened to him with respectful attention. He
stood out in his gray suit, grandiose, with his shoulders, the arch of
his shoulders, higher than everyone. Black binoculars hung on straps
at his stomach. Listening to the person talking to him, he put his
hands into his pockets and rocked quietly on his wide-spread legs
from heel to toe and toe to heel. He often scratches his nose. Having
scratched, he looks at his fingers which are in pinch formation and
brought close to his eyes. His listeners, like school children, involuntarily repeat his motions and the play of his face. They also scratch
their noses, wondering at themselves.

Infuriated, I walk away from them. I sat in the snack bar and,
caressed by the breeze off the field, drank beer. I prolonged the beer,
observing how the breeze sculptured delicate ornaments out of the
ends of the tablecloth of my table.

At the air terminal many miracles combined: here on the field
bloomed daisies, very near, by the barrier—ordinary, yellow-dust-
blowing daisies; here low, along the line of the horizon, rolled round
clouds resembling cannon smoke; here wooden arrows indicating
various directions glowed as the brightest red lead; here on high, con-
tracting and swelling, swayed a silk proboscis—the wind indicator;
and here along the grass, along the green grass of ancient battles, of
reindeer, of romance, crawled flying machines. I savored this taste,
these exquisite contrasts and combinations. The rhythm of the con-
tractions of the silk proboscis was conducive to contemplation.

Lucid, fluttering like the upper wing of an insect, the name Lilien-
thal since childhood years has sounded marvelous to me... Flying,
as if stretched on light bamboo laths, this name is connected in my
memory with the beginning of aviation. The flying man Otto Lilien-
thal was killed. Flying machines have stopped resembling birds. The
light wings transilluminated with yellow have been replaced by flip-
pers. You can see for yourself that they beat against the ground on
take-off. In any case, dust rises on take-off. Now a flying machine resembles a heavy fish. How quickly aviation has become an industry.

A march rang out. The People's Milcom arrived. Outstripping
his companions, the People's Milcom passed quickly along the path.

With the thrust and speed of his step he produced wind. Leaves rushed after him. The orchestra played smartly. The People's Milcom stepped smartly, all of him in rhythm with the orchestra.

I dashed to the gate, to the entrance to the field. But they held me back. A soldier said "not allowed" and put his hand on the upper edge of the gate.

"How's that?" I asked.

He turned away. His eyes fixed on the place where interesting events were unfolding. The pilot-designer in a ruddy leather jacket stood at attention in front of the People's Milcom. A strap tightly cinched the stocky back of the People's Milcom. They both held a salute. Everything was deprived of movement. Only the orchestra was all in movement. Babichev stood, sticking out his stomach.

"Let me pass, comrade!" I repeated, touching the soldier on the sleeve, and in answer heard:

"I'll remove you from the air terminal."

"But I was there. I only left for a minute. I'm with Babichev!"

It was necessary to show an invitation card. I didn't have one: Babichev simply dragged me along with him. Of course, I wouldn't have been disappointed at all even if I didn't get on the field. And here, behind the barrier, was an excellent place for observation. But I insisted. Something more significant than just the desire to see everything close up forced me to climb onto the wall. Suddenly I clearly realized my own incongruity to those who had been called to gather for the sake of this big and important event, the complete unnecessariness of my presence among them, the estrangement from everything that these people were doing—either here, on the field, or in any other place.

"Comrade, I'm not just a simple citizen," I became excited. (I couldn't have thought up a better sentence for the ordering of the jumble which was going on in my thoughts.) "What am I to you? A Philistine? Be so good as to let me pass. I'm from there." (I waved my hand at the group of people meeting the People's Milcom.)

"You're not from there," the soldier smiled.

"Ask Comrade Babichev!"

Into a megaphone made from my palms I shouted; I rose up on my toes:

"Andrei Petrovich!"

Just then the orchestra fell silent. The last beat of the drum ran off like a subterranean rumble.

"Comrade Babichev!"

He heard. The People's Milcom turned around too. Everyone turned around. The pilot raised his hand to his helmet, picturesquely, guarding against the sun.

Fear ran through me. I hung around somewhere behind the barrier; a potbellied person in pants that don't fit—how had I dared to distract them? And when silence ensued, when they, not yet having determined who was calling one of them, froze in expectant poses—I didn't find the strength in myself to call out another time.

But he knew, he saw, he heard that it was I calling him. A second—and everything ended. The group participants took their former poses. I was ready to cry.

Then I again rose up on my toes and through the same megaphone, deafening the soldier, sent a ringing howl in that unattainable direction:

"Sausage maker!"

And another time:

"Sausage maker!"

And many more times:

"Sausage maker! Sausage maker! Sausage maker!"

I saw only him, Babichev, towering above the rest with his Tyrolean hat. I remember the desire to close my eyes and sit down behind the barrier. I don't remember if I closed my eyes but if I did close them, then in any event I still managed to see the main thing. Babichev's face turned toward me. For one tenth of a second it remained turned toward me. There were no eyes. There were the two stupidly, mercurially shining plates of the pince-nez. Fear of some sort of immediate punishment plunged me into a state similar to sleep. I had a dream. So it seemed to me that I was sleeping. And the most frightful thing in that dream was that Babichev's head turned toward me on an immobile body, on its own axis, as on a screw. His back remained unturned.

X

I left the air terminal.

But the holiday clamoring there beckoned to me. I stopped on a green bank and stood, leaning against a tree, dustblown. The bushes surrounded me like a saint. I broke off the tender acidulous shoots and sucked on them. I stood, my kind, pale face raised, and looked at the sky.

A machine took off from the air terminal. With a frightful purr it sailed over me, yellow in the sun, aslope, like a signboard, almost tearing the leaves of my tree. Higher, higher—I followed it, stamping on the bank: it sped away, sometimes it flashed, sometimes it blackened. The distance was changing and it was changing, taking the forms of various objects: a rifle bolt, a quill pen, a trampled lilac blossom...

The celebration of the take-off of the new Soviet plane passed without me. War is declared. I insulted Babichev.

Right now they'll tumble out of the gates of the air terminal in a bunch. The chauffeurs were already exhibiting activity. There's Babichev's blue car. The chauffeur Alpers sees me, makes signs to me. I turn my back. My shoes got entangled in the green noodles of grass.

I have to talk with him. He has to understand. I have to explain to him that it's he who's to blame—that not I, but namely he's to blame. He won't come out alone. I have to talk with him face to face. From here he'll go to the office. I'll overtake him.

At the office they said that he was at the construction site right now.

"Two Bits?" Well then, to "Two Bits!"

Misfortune egged me on: as if some word which I had to say to him had already torn itself from my lips and I was chasing it, hurrying, afraid of not catching it, of losing and forgetting it.

The construction appeared to me as a yellowing mirage hanging in the air. There it is, "Two Bits!" It was behind houses, far away—separate parts of the scaffolding merged into one; like the lightest beehive it hovered in the distance.

I approached. Din and dust. I grow deaf and my cataracts begin to ache. I went along the wooden planking. A sparrow flew off a stump, the boards bent slightly, titillating with childhood memories of riding on a seesaw—I went, smiling at how the sawdust gathered and how my shoulders grew gray in the sawdust.

Where should I look for him?

A truck blocked the way. There's no way it can enter. It fidgets, rises and falls like a beetle crawling from a horizontal plane onto a vertical one.

The walks are entangled, just as if I'm walking in an ear.

"Comrade Babichev?"

They indicate that way. Somewhere they're banging out bilges.

"Where?"

"That way."

He's elusive.

He flashed by one time: his trunk passed over some kind of wooden siding. It disappeared. And now again he appears up above, far away—between us there's an enormous emptiness, all that which will soon be one of the building's courtyards.

He held up. There were still several others with him—caps, aprons. All the same, I'll call him in order to say one word: "Forgive."

They indicated the shortest way to that side. Only a ladder remained. I already hear the voices. Only a few rungs left to overcome...

But here's what happens. I have to bend down or else I'll be swept off. I bend down and grip a wooden rung with my hands. He flies over me. Yes, he shot past through the air.

In wild foreshortening I saw the figure flying in immobility—not the face, only the nostrils did I see: two holes, just as if I were looking up from below at a monument.

"What was this?"

I slid along the ladder.

He disappeared. He flew away. On an iron waffle he flew over to another place. The shadow of the grating accompanied his flight. He stood on an iron thing describing a semicircle with clanking and howling. What of it: a technical device, a crane. A platform of rail beams piled crosswise. Through the squared spaces I had seen his nostrils.

I sat down on the rung.

"Where is he?" I asked.

The workers around laughed and I smiled in all directions like a clown having concluded his performance with the most amazing fall from a horse.

"It's not I who's to blame," I said. "It's he who's to blame."

XI

I decided not to return to him.

My former dwelling already belonged to someone else. A lock hung on the door. The new inhabitant was absent. I remembered: in the face the widow Prokopovich resembles a padlock. Will she really enter my life again?

The night was spent on the boulevard. The most delightful morning expanded above me. A few more vagrants slept nearby on benches. They were lying doubled up, with their hands shoved into their sleeves and pressed to their stomach, resembling bound and be-headed Chinamen. Aurora touched them with cool fingers. They sighed, moaned, shook themselves and sat up, not opening their eyes and not disjoining their hands.

The birds awoke. Small sounds rang out: the small—among themselves—voices of birds, voices of grass. In a brick niche pigeons began to fidget.

Shaking, I rose. Yawning shook me like a dog.

(Gates were opening. A glass was filled with milk. Judges passed sentence. A man, having worked through the night, went up to a window and was surprised, not having recognized the street in the unusual light. A sick man asked for a drink. A boy ran into the kitchen to see if a mouse had been caught in the mousetrap. Morning began.)

On that day I wrote a letter to Andrei Babichev.

In the Palace of Labor on Solyanka I ate stuffed patties "Nelson," drank beer and wrote:

"Andrei Petrovich!"

"You sheltered me. You let me be by your side. I slept on your wonderful sofa. You know how wretchedly I lived before that. The blessed night came. You felt sorry for me, picked up a drunk.

"You surrounded me with linen sheets. It was as if the smooth-
ness and coldness of the material had been so calculated as to subdue
my intoxication, calm my agitation.

"In my life there even appeared the ivory buttons of a quilt cover and in them—just find the right point—swam the rainbow ring of
the spectrum. I recognized them immediately. They returned from
the long-since-forgotten, the farthest, the childhood corner of
memory.

"I got bedding."

This very word was such a particularly remote one for me, like
the word "ring-toss."

"You gave me bedding.

"From the heights of prosperity you lowered down onto me a
cloud of bedding, a halo, which clung to me with enchanting ardor,
blanketing me with memories, mild regrets and hopes. I began to
hope that still much of that which had been intended for my youth
might return.

"You indulged me, Andrei Petrovich!

"To think: a celebrated man brought me near to himself! A remarkable figure settled me in his house. I want to express my feelings
to you.

"Actually, just one feeling in all: hate.

"I hate you, Comrade Babichev.

"This letter is being written to knock some of the arrogance
out of you.

"From even the first days of my existence in your presence I
began to experience fear. You crushed me. You sat on me.

"You're standing in your shorts. The beery smell of sweat
spreads. I look at you and your face begins to enlarge strangely, your
torso enlarges—inflates, the clay of some sort of sculpture of an idol
protuberates. I'm ready to shout.

"Who gave him the right to crush me?

"How am I worse than he?

"Is he more intelligent?

"Richer in soul?

"More shrewdly organized?

"Stronger? More significant?

"Greater not only in position but also in essence?

"Why do I have to recognize his superiority?

"I put such questions to myself. Every day of observation gave me a fraction of the answer. A month passed. I know the answer. And I no longer fear you. You're simply a dull functionary. And nothing more. You didn't crush me with a significance of personality. Oh no! Now I already understand you clearly; having set you on my palm, I examine. My fear before you passed like some childishness. I've thrown you off me. You are a fake.

"At one time doubts tormented me. 'Perhaps I'm a nonentity compared to him?' I thought. 'Perhaps for me, for an ambitious man, he is indeed an example of a great man?'

"But it turned out that you're simply a functionary, ignorant and dull, like all functionaries who were before you and will be after you. And like all functionaries you're a two-bit tyrant. Only by two-bit tyranny can the hurricane which you raised around a piece of mediocre sausage or the fact that you brought home an unknown young man off the street be explained. And perhaps out of the same two-bit tyranny you brought near to yourself Volodya Makarov, about whom I know only one thing, that he is a soccer player. You are a lord. You need jesters and hangers-on. I don't doubt that this Volodya Makarov ran away from you, not having endured the derision. It must be that just like me, you were systematically turning him into a fool.

"You announced that he lived in your presence like a son, that he saved your life; you were even overcome with reverie remembering him. I remember. But this is all a lie. It's uncomfortable to recognize lordly leanings in yourself. But I saw the birthmark you have on your waist.

"At first, when you said that the sofa belonged to that one and that on his return I would have to cast myself to the devil's mother—I took offense. But I understood in a minute that both to him and to me you're cold and impersonal. You are a lord, we are hangers-on.

"But I dare assure you, neither he nor I—we won't return to you any more. You don't respect people. He'll return only in the event that he's more stupid than I.

"My fate turned out such that there's neither penal servitude nor a revolutionary record behind me. They won't entrust to me such responsible business as the preparation of sparkling waters or the construction of apiaries.

"But does this mean that I am a poor son of the century and you a good one? Does this mean that I am a nothing and you a big something?

"You found me on the street...

"How stupidly you behaved!

" 'On the street,' you decided, 'well , all right, a gray personality, let him work. A proofreader, then, a proofreader, a correcter, a reader, all right.' You didn't condescend to a young man off the street. Here your rapture told on itself. You are a functionary, Comrade Babichev.

"Who did you think I was? A dying Lumpenproletarian? Did you decide to maintain me? Thank you. I'm strong—do you hear?— I'm so very strong, as to die and to rise up and to die again.

"I wonder how you'll act having read my letter. Perhaps you'll try to have them deport me or perhaps you'll put me in an insane asylum? You can do anything, you are a great person, a member of the government. You said of your own brother that he should be shot. You said: we'll put him in Konatchikov.

"Your brother, who makes an unusual impression, is enigmatic to me, incomprehensible. Here there's a secret, here I don't understand anything. The name 'Ophelia' excites me strangely. And you, it seems to me, are afraid of this name.

"I'm making some conjecture all the same. I foresee something. I'll hinder you. Yes, I'm almost sure that this is so. I won't allow you. You want to capture your brother's daughter. Only one time did I see her. Yes, it was I who told her about the bough full of flowers and leaves. You don't have an imagination. You ridiculed me. I heard the telephone conversation. You slandered me in the girl's eyes the same as you slandered him, her father. It's unfavorable for you to allow that the girl whom you want to subjugate, to make into a fool in your presence, as you tried to make us into fools—that this girl should have a tender, agitated soul. You want to utilize her, as you utilize (I purposely employ your word) 'heads and hooves of sheep with the aid of cleverly employed electric, spiral drills' (from your brochure).

"But no, I won't allow you. Certainly: what a dainty morsel! You're a glutton and a gourmandizer. Will you really stop at anything for the sake of your physiology? What's keeping you from corrupting the girl? The fact that she's your niece? But you laugh at family, at origin. You'd like to tame her.

"And therefore you inveigh against your brother with such fury. But anyone would say, having barely glanced at him: this is a remarkable man. I think, not yet knowing him: he's brilliant, in what—I don't know... You persecute him. I heard how you banged your fist against the railing. You forced daughter to leave father.

"But you won't persecute me.

"I'm coming to the defense of your brother and his daughter. Listen, you dullard who laughed at the bough full of flowers and leaves, listen—yes, only thus, only with this exclamation am I able to express my ecstasy at the sight of her. But what sort of words are you preparing for her? You called me an alcoholic only because I addressed the girl in figurative language incomprehensible to you. The incomprehensible is either funny or frightful. Right now you're laughing, but I'll soon force you to be horrified. Don't worry, not only figuratively—I know how to think quite really. Why not! I can speak about her, about Volodya, in usual words too—and here, if you please, I'll cite for you right now a series of attributives comprehensible to you, intentionally, in order to rouse you, to tease with that which you won't get, respected sausage maker.

"Yes, she stood before me—yes, first I'll tell it my way: she was lighter than a shadow, the very lightest of shadows—the shadow of falling snow could envy her; yes, first my way: not with her ear did she listen to me but with her temple, lightly tilting her head; yes, her face resembles a nut: in color—because of the tan, and in form—with cheek bones rounded and tapering toward the chin. Is this comprehensible to you? No? So here's more. From running, her dress was disarranged, opened, and I saw: she's still not completely covered with tan, on her breast I saw the pale blue fork of a vein...

"And now—your way. A description of the one whom you

want to regale. Before me stood a girl sixteen years of age, almost a
little girl, broad in the shoulders, gray-eyed, with close-cut and tousled
hair—a charming juvenile built like a chess figure (this is already my
way!), not too tall.

"You won't get her.

"She will be my wife. I've dreamed about her my whole life.

"We'll go to war! We'll battle! You're thirteen years older than
I. They are behind you and ahead of me. Yet one other achievement
in the sausage business, yet one other low price cafeteria—here are
the limits of your activity.

"Oh, I dream of something else!

"Not you—I'll get Valya. We'll thunder in Europe—there, where
they love glory.

"I'll get Valya—as a prize—for everything: for the humiliations,
for the youth which I didn't have time to see, for my dog's life.

"I told you about the cook. Remember: about how she washes
in the corridor. Now then, I'll see something else: a room somewhere
will sometime be brightly illuminated by the sun, a blue basin will
stand by the window, the window will dance in the basin and Valya
will wash over the basin, sparkling like a mirror-carp, will splash, will
finger the keyboard of water...

"In order that this dream be fulfilled I'll do everything! You
won't take advantage of Valya.

"Good-bye, Comrade Babichev!

"How could I have played such a humiliating role for a whole
month? I won't return to you any more. Wait: perhaps your first fool
will return. Give him my regards. What happiness that I won't return
to you any more.

"Every time when my self-esteem will suffer from something,
then I'll know that just then, by the association of ideas, a certain
of those evenings spent close to your desk will be recalled to me.
What painful visions!

"Evening. You're at the desk. Self-esteem radiates from you.
'I'm working,' these rays chatter, 'do you hear, Kavalerov, I'm working, don't disturb...tss...Philistine.'

"And in the morning praise rushes from various mouths:

" 'A great man! A marvelous man! A perfect personality—

Andrei Petrovich Babichev.'

"But now at that time when sycophants were singing hymns to you, at that time when self-satisfaction puffed you up, lived next to you a man whom no one considered and of whom no one asked an opinion; lived a man following after each of your movements, studying you, observing you—not from below, not servilely, but humanely, calmly—and coming to the conclusion that you are a high ranking official—and only that, a commonplace personality raised to an enviable height thanks solely to external conditions.

"There's no reason to play the fool.

"That's everything I wanted to tell you.

"You wanted to make a jester out of me—I became your enemy. 'Against whom are you waging war, scoundrel?' you shouted to your brother. I don't know whom you had in mind: yourself, your party, your factories, stores, apiaries—I don't know. But I'm waging war against you: against the most ordinary lord, egoist, sensualist and dullard, assured that everything will come off all right for him. I am waging war for your brother, for the girl who has been deceived by you, for tenderness, for pathos, for personality, for names which are disturbing, like the name 'Opheila,' for everything which you suppress, remarkable man. Give my regards to Solomon Shapiro..."

XII

The cleaning woman let me in. Babichev's already gone. The traditional milk is drunk. On the table is a cloudy glass. Next to it is a plate with cookies resembling Hebrew letters.

Human life is insignificant. The movement of worlds is formidable. When I settled here a solar hare sat on the door jamb at two o'clock in the afternoon. Thirty-six days passed. The hare jumped into another room. The earth passed the recurrent part of its path. The solar hare, a child's toy, reminds us of eternity.

I went out onto the balcony. On the corner a small group of people were listening to the church chime. There was chiming in a church not visible from the balcony. This church is famed for its bellringer.

Idlers threw back their heads. The work of the famous bellringer was visible to them.

Once I, too, stood a good hour on the corner. In the reaches of an arch opened the interior of the bell tower. There in the sooty darkness, the sort found in garrets, among the garret girders shrouded with cobweb, raged the bellringer. Twenty bells tore at him. Like a coachman he leaned back, bent his head, perhaps, shrieked. He writhed at a middle point, in the center of a gloomy cobweb of ropes, then stopped dead, hanging by extended arms, then threw himself into a corner, distorting the whole sketch of the cobweb—the mysterious musician, indistinguishable, black, perhaps deformed like Quasimodo.

(By the way, the distance painted him as frightful as that. With the desire it could be told this way too: a little fellow is putting away dishes, plates. And to call the chime of the famous bell tower a mixture of restaurant and railroad station clatter.)

I listened from the balcony.

"Tom-vir-lir-li! Tom-vir-lir-li! Tom-vir-lir-li!"

Tom Virlirli. Some Tom Virlirli hovered in the air.

> *Tom Virlirli,*
> *Tom with knapsack hung,*
> *Tom Virlirli is young!*

The tousled bellringer put many of my mornings to music. Tom—the stroke of a big bell, a big caldron. Virlirli—small saucers.

Tom Virlirli passed into me on one of the fine mornings met by me in this shelter. The musical phrase turned into a verbal one. I pictured this Tom to myself vividly.

A youth viewing the city. A youth known to no one has already arrived, is already near, already sees the city which sleeps and suspects nothing. The morning fog is just dissipating. The city billows in the valley through a shimmering, green cloud. Tom Virlirli, smiling and pressing his hand to his heart, looks at the city searching for outlines familiar from childhood pictures.

A knapsack is on the youth's back.

He'll do everything.

It is he who is the very arrogance of youth, the very concealment of proud dreams.

Days will pass—and soon (not many times will the solar hare

skip from the jamb into the other room) boys, themselves dreaming also to pass with a knapsack on their back on a May morning through the outskirts of the city, through the outskirts of glory, will sing a little song about a man who did what he wanted to do:

> *Tom Virlirli,*
> *Tom with knapsack hung,*
> *Tom Virlirli is young!*

Thus the chime of an ordinary Moscow church turned inside me into a romantic dream of obviously Western-European character.

I'll leave the letter on the desk, collect my belongings (in a knapsack?) and leave. I put the letter, folded into a square, on the glass plate adjacent to the portrait of the one whom I consider my comrade in misfortune.

There is a knock at the door. He?

I opened.

In the door, holding a knapsack in his hand, smiling gaily (with a Japanese smile), as if having seen through the door a good friend cherished in dreams, shy, in some way resembling Valya, stood Tom Virlirli.

This was the dark-complexioned youth, Volodya Makarov. He looked at me with surprise and then circled the room with his eyes. Several times his glance returned to the sofa, downward, under the sofa, where my shoes were in sight.

"Hullo!" I greeted him.

He went to the sofa, sat down, sat awhile, then headed into the bedroom, stayed there awhile, returned, and stopping by the flamingo vase, asked me:

"Where's Andrei Petrovich? At the office?"

"I'm not sure. Andrei Petrovich will return in the evening. It's possible he'll bring a new fool with him. You're the first, I'm the second and he'll be the third. Or were there already fools before you? But it's possible he'll bring the girl with him."

"Whom?" asked Tom Virlirli. "What's that?" he asked frowning from incomprehension. His temples rose.

He sat down on the sofa again. The shoes under the sofa disturbed him. It was evident: he would've been glad to touch them with the back of his boot.

"Why did you return?" I asked. "Why the devil did you return?

Our role is finished. Right now he's busy with someone else. He's seducing a girl. His niece, Valya. Understand? Get out of here. Listen!"

(I threw myself at him. He sat motionless.)

"Listen! Do what I did! Tell him the whole truth... Here (I grabbed the letter from the table), here's a letter that I wrote to him..."

He pushed me aside. Out of habit the knapsack settled in the corner near the sofa. He went to the telephone and called the office.

And so my belongings remained uncollected.

I fled.

XIII

The letter remained with me. I decided to destroy it. The soccer player lived in his presence like a son. By the way the knapsack established itself in the corner, by the way he looked over the room, removed the telephone receiver and cited the number, it was evident: he's of long standing, he's at home in the house—this is his house. The badly spent night was influencing me. I didn't write what I wanted to write. Babichev wouldn't have understood my indignation. He would have explained it as envy. He would have thought I envy Volodya.

It's good that the letter remained with me.

Otherwise it would have come off a blank shot.

I was mistaken thinking that Volodya was a fool in his presence and an entertainer. Consequently, I shouldn't have taken him under defense in my letter. On the contrary. Now, having met him, I've seen his arrogance. Babichev is cultivating and cherishing one similar to himself. The same sort of haughty and blind person will spring up.

His look said: "Excuse me, you were mistaken. A hanger-on— that's you. But I am an equal. I am a young lord."

I was sitting on a bench. And here something horrible was revealed.

The little square turned out to be the wrong one—mine was bigger; this is not my letter. Mine remained there. In haste I had grabbed another letter. Here it is:

"Dear, kind Andrei Petrovich! Hello, hello! Are you in good

[44]

health? Hasn't your new tenant choked you? Hasn't Ivan Petrovich set 'Ophelia' on you? Take care: they'll both conspire—your Kavalerov and Ivan Petrovich—and exterminate you. Take care, beware. Because you're weak, it's easy to insult you, you take care...

"Why have you become so trusting? You're letting all sorts of riff-raff into the house. Drive him to the devil. On the very next day you should have said: 'Well, you've slept it off, young man, and so good-bye!' Think of it: coddling! When I'd read your letter where, you say, you remembered about me and felt sorry for a drunk on the curb, picked him up and led him away for my sake, because, you say, somewhere a misfortune might happen to me too and that I would be lying like that—when I'd read this—it became funny and incomprehensible to me. This isn't like you but Ivan Petrovich.

"It came out just as I suggested: you brought this cunning culprit home and then lost your head, of course—you yourself don't know what to do with him. And it's awkward to ask him to clear out, and what to do—the devil only knows! Right? You see: I'm moralizing to you. Your work is such, it disposes you to sentimentality: fruits, herbs, bees and everything like that. But I'm an industrial man. Laugh, laugh, Andrei Petrovich! You're always laughing at me. I, you understand, am already a new generation.

"How will it be now? Well, I'll return—what will happen with your eccentric? And what if your eccentric bursts into tears and doesn't want to get off the sofa? And you'll even feel sorry for him. Yes, I'm jealous. I'll drive him out, pound his puss. You're just so kind, you only shout, bang your fist, get ruffled, but when it comes to business, you're right there—to feel sorry. If it wasn't for me, Valya would still be tormenting herself at Ivan Petrovich's. How are you keeping her down? She hasn't gone back? You yourself know: Ivan Petrovich is a cunning man, he pretends, even says of himself that he's a trifle and a charlatan. Right? So don't feel sorry for him.

"Just try to set him up in a dispensary. He'll run away. Or propose to Kavalerov to go to a dispensary. He'll be insulted.

"Well, all right. Don't you be angry. After all your words were: 'Teach me, Volodya, and I will teach you.' And so you were learning.

"I'll arrive soon. In the next few days. Daddy sends you his regards. Farewell, Murom—small town! At night, when I'm walking along, then I understand that strictly speaking the town doesn't exist

at all. There are only workshops, but a small town—what's this! It's
so simple, an accumulation of workshops. All for them, for their sake.
Workshops above everything. At night in the town there's an Egyptian
darkness, gloom, you understand, goblins. And to the side, in the field,
the workshops blaze with lamps, beam—a holiday.

"And in the town (I saw) a calf was running after the district
inspector, after the briefcase (which he held under his arm). It runs,
smacking its lips, perhaps it wanted to chew or something... Such a
picture: a hedge, a puddle, the inspector strides out in a red cap, in
proper fashion, and a calf aims at his briefcase. A contradiction, you
understand.

"I don't like these very calves. I am a man-machine. You won't
recognize me. I've turned into a machine. If I haven't already turned,
then I want to turn. The machines here are beasts. Thoroughbreads!
Remarkably indifferent, proud machines. Not what's in your sausage
works. You're using primitive means. You only have to cut up calves.
I want to be a machine. I want to consult with you. I want to become
proud from work, proud because I work. In order to be indifferent,
you understand, to everything that's not work! Envy toward the machine has taken hold—that's what it is! How am I worse than it? We
invented it, created it, but it turned out much more ferocious than
we. Give it a start—it's away! It'll work so that there's not a squiggle
extra. And I too want to be like that. You understand, Andrei Petrovich—so there's not a squiggle extra. How I'd like to talk with you.

"I imitate you in everything. I even chomp like you in imitation.

"How many times I think about how I lucked out. You understood me, Andrei Petrovich! Not all young Communists live this way.
And I live in your presence, in the presence of a most wise, a marvelous personality. Anyone would give a lot for such a life. I know it:
many envy me. Thank you, Andrei Petrovich! Don't you laugh—I'm
confessing love, you say. A machine, you'll say, and he's confessing
love. Right? No, I'm telling the truth: I will be a machine.

"How are things? Is 'Two Bits' being built? Nothing collapsed,
did it? How's 'Warmth and Strength'? Did you settle it? And Kampfer?

"And what about at home? So then an unknown citizen is sleeping on that little sofa of mine? He'll bring lice. Remember how they
hauled me off from the soccer match. It still echoes. Remember, they

carried me? And you got scared, Andrei Petrovich? So you really got scared? You're my slobberer! I was lying on the sofa; my leg's heavy as a rail. Myself looking at you—you're at the desk behind a green lamp shade, writing. I'm loking at you—and suddenly you at me; I close me eyes immediately—like with Mama.

"Speaking about soccer. I'll be playing against the Germans on the Moscow combined team. And, perhaps, if Shukhov doesn't—on the combined team of the U. S. S. R. Splendid!

"How's Valka? Of course we'll get married! In four years. You laugh, you say—we won't make it. But I here declare to you: in four years. Yes. I'll be the Edison of the new century. I'll kiss her for the first time when your 'Two Bits' opens. Yes. You don't believe it? I have a pact with her. You don't know anything. On the day of the opneing of the 'Two Bits' we'll kiss on the tribunal as the music plays.

"Don't you forget me, Andrei Petrovich. Suppose I arrive and this is what turns out: your Kavalerov is your best friend, I'm forgotten about and he's taken my place for you. He does gymnastics together with you, goes to the construction site. All sorts of things? And maybe he turned out to be a remarkable guy, much more pleasant than I—maybe you became friends with him and I, Edison of the new century, will have to get the hell out. Maybe you're sitting with him and with Ivan Petrovich and with Valka—and you're laughing at me? And Kavalerov's married Valka? Tell the truth. Then I'll kill you, Andrei Petrovich. Word of honor. For the betrayal of our talks, plans. Understand?

"Well, I've written a lot, I'm disturbing a busy man. So that there wouldn't be a squiggle extra—but even this got out of hand. It's because we're apart—true? Well, good-bye, dear and respected, good-bye, we'll see each other soon."

XIV

A huge cloud with the outline of South America stood over the city. It shone, but the shadow from it was threatening. Astronomically slowly the shadow moved onto Babichev's street.

Everyone who had already entered the orifice of that street and was walking against the current saw the movement of the shadow, everything went dark before their eyes, it took the ground from under their feet. They were walking as if on a revolving sphere.

I made my way together with them.

The balcony hung. On the railing—a jacket. They were no longer chiming at the church. I replaced the idlers on the corner. A youth appeared on the balcony. The approaching cloudiness surprised him. He raised his head, looked out, leaning over the railing.

Stairs, a door. I knock. My lapel twitches from the beating of my heart. I came to fight.

They let me in. The one who opened the door for me steps aside drawing the door toward himself. And the first that I see is Andrei Babichev. Andrei Babichev is standing in the middle of the room having spread his legs, under which an army of Lilliputians ought to pass. His hands are thrust in his trouser pockets. His jacket is unbuttoned and gathered behind. Because his hands are in his pockets the skirts along both sides in the back form scallops. His pose says:

"We-ll, sir?"

I see only him. Volodya Makarov I only hear,

I step toward Babichev. It's raining.

Any second I'll fall down on my knees before him.

"Don't chase me out! Andrei Petrovich, don't chase me out! I understood everything. Believe me like you believe Volodya. Believe me: I'm also young, I'll also be the Edison of the new century, I'll also idolize you! How could I have missed it, how could I have been so blind not to do everything so that you'd have grown fond of me! Forgive me, let me, give me four years' time..."

But without falling on my knees I ask maliciously:

"Why aren't you at work?"

"Get out of here!" I hear in answer.

He answered immediately, just as if we were rehearsing. But the cue reached my consciousness after a certain interval of time.

Something extraordinary happened.

It was raining. It's possible there was lightning.

I don't want to talk figuratively. I want to talk simply. Once I read "Atmosphere" by Camille Flammarion. (What a planetary name! Flammarion—it's a veritable star.) He describes spherical lightning, its marvelous effect: a full smooth sphere soundlessly rolls into a space, filling it with blinding light... Oh, I'm so far from the intent to resort to commonplace comparisons. But the cloud was suspicious. But the shadow moved as in a dream. But it was raining. In the bedroom the window was open. You shouldn't leave windows open in a thunderstorm! There's a draft!

From the bedroom, together with the rain, with the drops bitter like tears, with the gusts of wind in which the flamingo vase runs like a flame igniting the curtains which likewise run under the ceiling, appears Valya.

But this appearance stuns only me. As a matter of fact it's all simple: a friend arrived and his friends hurried to see him.

It's possible Babichev went by for Valya, who was dreaming, possibly, of this very day. It's all simple. I have to be sent to the dispensary to be cured by hypnosis so that I won't think in images and won't ascribe the effects of spherical lightning to a girl.

So I'll spoil simplicity for you.

"Get out of here!" my hearing repeats.

"It's not all so simple..." I begin.

It's drafty. The door remained open. Because of the wind one wing grew on me. It spins madly over my shoulder blowing against my eyelids. Half my face is anesthetized by the draft.

"It's not all so simple," I say pressing against the door jamb in order to break the horrible wing. "You went away, Volodya, and during that time Comrade Babichev was living with Valya. While you'll be there waiting four years, Andrei Petrovich will manage to treat himself to Valya to a sufficient degree..."

I found myself behind the door. Half of my face was anesthetized. Perhaps I didn't feel the blow.

The lock clicked above me just as though a twig broke, and I fell from the beautiful tree like an overripe, lazy fruit, spattering on the fall.

"It's all over," I said calmly, rising. "Now I'll kill you, Comrade Babichev."

XV

It's raining.

The rain walks along Color Boulevard, rambles through the circus, turns onto the boulevards on the right and, having reached Petrovsky Heights, suddenly goes blind and loses confidence.

I cross "The Horn" thinking about the fabulous fencer who walked in the rain repelling the drops with his foil. The foil sparkled, the skirts of his doublet fluttered, the fencer twisted, bobbed like a flute—and stayed dry. He received his father's inheritance. I got soaked to the ribs and, it seems, received a slap in the face.

I find that a landscape observed through the distancing lenses of binoculars gains in lustre, vividness and stereoscopy. Colors and contours sort of sharpen. A thing, remaining a familiar thing, suddenly becomes small, unusual to the point of absurdity. This calls forth childish notions in the observer. Just as if you're dreaming. Take note how a man having turned binoculars to distancing begins to smile delightedly.

After the rain the city acquired lustre and stereoscopy. Everyone saw it: the trolley is painted carmine; the cobbles of the pavement are not monochromatic, there are even green ones among them; a house painter on high came out of the niche where he'd hidden from the rain like a pigeon and walked along a canvas of bricks; a boy in a window catches the sun on a fragment of mirror...

I bought an egg and a French roll from an old woman. I struck the egg against the trolley stop post in the sight of passengers rushing from Petrovsky Gates.

I set out uphill. Benches passed on the level of my knees. Here the avenue is somewhat convex. Beautiful mothers were sitting on the benches having laid out their kerchiefs. On the suntan covered faces eyes shone—with the light of fish scales. Suntan likewise covered both necks and shoulders. But the big, young breasts visible in the blouses showed white. Lonely and exhausted, I drank with melancholy this whiteness whose name was—milk, motherhood, matrimony, pride and purity.

A nurse held an infant resembling in vesture the Pope of Rome.

A little girl in a red hairband had a sunflower seed hanging on her lip. The girl was listening the the orchestra without having noticed how she'd gotten into a puddle. The bells of the bass horns looked like elephant ears.

For everyone: for the mothers, for the nurses, for the girls, for the musicians entangled in pipes, I was—a comic. The trumpeters squinted at me puffing up their cheeks even more. The little girl chuckled, because of which the sunflower seed finally fell. Then and there she discovered the puddle. She blamed me for her own misfortune and turned away with malice.

I'll prove that I'm not a comic. No one understands me. The incomprehensible seems funny or frightful. It'll become frightful for everyone.

I went up to a street mirror.

I like street mirrors every much. They arise unexpectedly across your route. Your route is usual, calm—a usual urban route promising neither miracles nor visions. You walk along not surmising anything, raise your eyes and suddenly, in an instant, it becomes clear to you: unprecedented changes have taken place with the world, with the rules of the world.

Destroyed are optics, geometry, destroyed is the nature of that which was your walk, your movement, your desire to go precisely there to where you were going. You begin to think that you see with the back of your head—you even smile embarrassedly at the passers-by, you're confused by your advantage.

"Oh..." you sigh quietly.

A trolley which has just become hidden from your eyes, rushes again before you, cutting along the edge of the boulevard like a knife along a cake. A straw hat hanging on an azure ribbon over someone's arm (just this minute you saw it, it attracted your attention, but you didn't have the time to look around) returns to you and floats by across your eyes.

The distance opens before you. Everyone's sure: that's a house, a wall, but to you has been given the advantage: that's not a house! You've discovered a mystery: here's not a wall, here's a mysterious world where everything you've just seen repeats and at the same time repeats with that stereoscopy and vividness which is subject only to the distancing lenses of binoculars.

You, as it's said, are hung up. So sudden is the destruction of rules, so improbable the change of proportions. But you rejoice at the dizziness... Having guessed, you hurry to the azure square. Your face hangs motionless in the mirror, it alone has natural forms, it alone is a particle remaining from the regular world at the time when everything collapsed, changed and acquired a new regularity with which you can't get comfortable having stood at least a whole hour in front of the mirror where your face is just as if in a tropical garden. Too green the greenery, too blue the sky.

You couldn't say for sure (until you turned away from the mirror) in which direction a pedestrian seen by you in the mirror is heading... Only having turned...

Chewing up the roll I looked into the mirror.

I turned away.

Appearing somewhere from the side, a pedestrian walked toward the mirror. I prevented him from being reflected. The smile which he'd prepared for himself fell to me. He was a head shorter than I and raised his head.

He was hurrying to the mirror in order to find and knock off a caterpillar which had fallen onto a distant part of his shoulder. He knocked it off with a flick, having turned out his shoulder like a violinist.

I continued to think about optical illusions, about the trick of the mirror, and for that reason asked the one who'd approached, still not having recognized him:

"From which direction did you approach? Where did you come from?"

"From where?" he answered. "Where did I come from?" (He looked at me with clear eyes.) "I myself invented me."

He took off his derby uncovering a bald spot and made an exaggeratedly smart bow. In the way has-beens greet an alms giver. And as of a has-been, bags drooped under his eyes like lilac stockings. He sucked candy.

At once I realized: here's my friend and teacher and comforter.

I grabbed him by the arm and almost falling against him began to say:

"Tell me, answer me!..."

He raised his eyebrows.

"What is this...'Ophelia?' "

He was about to answer. But through the corner of his lips burst a flux of hard candy as sweet juice. Feeling excitement and rapture, I waited for his answer.

PART TWO

I

The approach of old age did not frighten Ivan Babichev. Sometimes, however, complaints were heard from his lips with regard to swiftly flowing life, lost years, supposed cancer of the stomach... But his complaints were too light, in all probability, not even very sincere—complaints of a rhetorical character.

He used to put his palm on the left side of his chest, smile and ask:

"I wonder what kind of sound occurs on the rupturing of a heart?"

Once he raised his hand showing his friends the outward side of his palm where the veins were arranged in the form of a tree and burst out with the following improvisation:

"Here," he uttered, "is the tree of life. Here is the tree which tells me more about life and death than the blooming and withering trees of gardens. I don't remember exactly when I discovered that my hand blooms like a tree.... But it must have been at the fine time when the blooming and the withering of the trees spoke to me not about life and death but about the end and the beginning of the academic year! It showed blue then, this tree, it was blue and slender and the blood, which I then imagined was not liquid but light, rose over it like the dawn and endowed the whole landscape of the metacarpus with a similarity to a Japanese water color...

"Years passed, I changed and the tree changed.

[57]

"I remember a magnificent time—it branched out. I experienced pride seeing its irresistible blooming. It became rough and brown and in that, might was concealed. I could call it the mighty rigging of my hand. But now, my friends! How decrepit it is, how rotten!

"It seems to me that the branches are breaking, that hollows have appeared... This is sclerosis, my friends! And that the skin is suffering and under it the tissue is becoming watery—is that not the setting of fog on the tree of my life, of fog which will soon shroud all of me?"

There were three Babichev brothers. Ivan was the second. The oldest was called Roman. He was a member of a militant organization and was executed for participation in a terrorist act.

The youngest brother—Andrei—lived in emigration. "How do you like it, Andrei?" Ivan wrote to him in Paris. "We have a martyr in the family! How glad Grandma would have been!" To which brother Andrei with his peculiar rudeness answered briefly: "You're simply a scoundrel." Thus formed the discord between the brothers.

Since childhood Ivan astonished family and acquaintances.

As a twelve-year-old boy he demonstrated in the family circle an apparatus of strange appearance, something like a lamp shade with a fringe of jingles, and assured that with the aid of his apparatus it was possible to evoke in anyone—by order—any dream.

"Fine," said his father, the director of a gymnasium and a latinist. "I believe you. I want to have a dream out of Roman history."

"What exactly?" the boy asked businesslike.

"It's all the same. The Battle of Pharsalus. But if it doesn't work out, I'll whip you."

Late in the evening a wonderful ringing flashed, rushing throughout the rooms. The director of the gymnasium lay in the study, flat and straight with malice, as in a coffin. The mother hovered at the irritably closed doors. Little Vanya, smiling good naturedly, strolled along the sofa brandishing his lamp shade as a tightrope-walker brandishes a Chinese umbrella. In the morning the father, undressed, darted in three jumps from the study into the nursery and pulled the fat, kind, sleepy, lazy Vanya out of bed. The day was still faint, something might still come of it, but the director rent the curtains, spuriously greeting the coming of morning. The mother wanted to prevent the thrashing, the mother slipped her hands in, shouted:

"Don't beat him, Petenka, don't beat... He made a mistake... Word of honor... So what if you didn't dream?.. The ringing took off in another direction. You know what kind of an apartment we have... damp. I, I saw the battle of Pharsalus! I dreamed about the battle, Petenka."

"Don't lie," said the director. "Relate the details. By what was the uniform of the Balearic archers distinguished from the uniform of the Numidian slingers?.. Well?"

He waited a minute, the mother sobbed and the little experimenter was thrashed. He behaved like Galileo. In the evening of the same day the maid informed her mistress that she would not marry a certain Dobrodeyev who had proposed to her.

"He lies all the time, it's impossible to believe him," so the maid explained. "All night I saw horses. They all gallop, all frightful horses, sort of in masks. And to see a horse is a lie."

Losing control of her lower jaw the mother, like a lunatic, went to the door of the study. The cook froze at the stove feeling that she also was losing control of her lower jaw.

The wife touched the husband's shoulder. He was sitting at the desk attaching to his cigarette case the monogram which had fallen off.

And the mother babbled:

"Petrusha, Frosya... It seems Frosya dreamed about the battle of Pharsalus."

It's unknown how the director regarded the maid's dream. Concerning Ivan, it's known that a month or two after the episode with the artificial dreams he was already telling about his new invention.

It seems he invented a special soap compound and a special little pipe, using which, one could turn out an amazing soap bubble. This bubble would enlarge in flight achieving in turn the dimensions of a Christmas tree ornament, of a ball, and then of a sphere the size of a summerhouse flower bed, and on, on, right up to the volume of an aerostat—and then it would burst, pouring over the city a short golden rain.

The father was in the kitchen. (He belonged to the gloomy species of fathers priding themselves on a knowledge of some culinary secrets and considering as their exceptional privilege, say, the determining of the amount of bay leaves necessary for some soup illustrious by legacy or, say, the supervision of the time spent in a pan by eggs for which it's proscribed to achieve the ideal state—so called 'poached eggs.')

Outside the kitchen window in the little yard right next to the wall little Ivan was indulging in daydreams. The father was listening with his yellow ear and looked out. Boys surrounded Ivan. And Ivan was lying about the soap bubble. It'll be big as a balloon.

The bile seethed anew in the director. The eldest son, Roman, had left the family a year ago. The father was taking it out on the younger ones.

God insulted him with sons.

He recoiled from the window even smiling with spite. During dinner he awaited Ivan's statement, but Ivan didn't give voice. "It seems he despises me. It seems he considers me a fool," boiled the director. And at the close of the day when father Babichev was drinking tea on the balcony, suddenly somewhere very far away above the very dwindling, hyaline, back plane of his field of vision, lively and yellowishly gleaming in the rays of the sun, appeared a large orange sphere. It floated slowly, crossing the plane on an oblique line.

The director darted into the room and immediately, through the span of the door, he saw Ivan on the windowsill in the next room. Completely fixed toward the window the school boy loudly clapped his hands.

"I got complete satisfaction on that day," Ivan Petrovich recalled. "Father was frightened. For a long time after I sought his gaze, but he hid his eyes. And I began to pity him. He blackened—I thought he'd die. And generously I threw off the cloak. He was a dry man, my dad, small-minded, but inattentive. He didn't know that on that day the aeronaut, Ernst Vitallo, flew over the city. Magnificent posters announced about it. I confessed to involuntary deception. I have to tell you that my experiments with soap bubbles didn't lead to those results about which I dreamed.

(The facts say that at the time when Ivan Babichev was a twelve-year-old school boy aerostatics had not yet achieved widespread development and it's doubtful that flights over provincial towns were organized in those days.

But if this is a fib—so what! A fib—that's reason's beloved.)

Friends listened to Ivan Babichev's improvisations with delight.

"And it seems to me that at night, after that distressing day, my dad saw the Battle of Pharsalus in a dream. He didn't go to school in the morning. Mom brought him mineral water in the study. In all probability the details of the battle shook him. It might be that he couldn't be reconciled with that mockery of history in which the dream indulged... It's possible that he dreamed that the Balearic slingers decided the outcome of the battle arriving in balloons..."

With such an ending Ivan Babichev concluded his tale about soap bubbles.

Another time he shared with friends such an incident from the epoch of his adolescence:

"A student by the name of Shemiot was courting a young lady... and what's worse—I don't remember the young lady's name... let's say they called the young lady Lilia Kapitanaki who clicked her heels like a goat. What went on in the yard was known to all of us boys. The student languished under Lilia's balcony ready and afraid to call forth from the golden entrails of the balcony door this girl who had reached sixteen and who seemed to us boys an old woman.

"The student's cap showed blue, the student's cheeks showed red. The student arrived on a bicycle. And indescribable was the student's grief when on a Sunday in May, on one of those Sunday's of which no more than ten are innumerated in the monuments of meteorological science, on a Sunday, when the breeze was so nice and caressing that one felt like tying a blue ribbon around it, dashing up to the balcony, the student saw Lilia's aunt leaning with her elbows on the railing, parti-colored and flowered like the slip cover on an armchair in a provincial parlor—all in twists, crescents and frills and with a hairdo resembling a snail. And the aunt rejoiced evidently at the appearance of the student Shemiot—from the height she threw open, one might say, an embrace to the student and proclaimed in a potato voice, in a voice so wetted with saliva and full of tongue, just as if she were talking while chewing something hot:

" 'Lilechka's leaving for Herson. Leaving today. At seven-forty. Leaving for a long time. Leaving for the whole summer. She told me to say "bye" to you, Sergei Sergeyevich, "Bye." ' "

"But the student with a lover's scent understood everything.

He knew that in the golden depth of the room Lilechka was sobbing and that Lilechka was straining toward the balcony and without seeing, saw the student whose tunic, being white, absorbed into itself according to the laws of physics the greatest number of rays and shone with a blinding, Alpine whiteness—but it was impossible to escape, for the aunt was all-powerful.

" 'Give me your bicycle and I'll avenge you,' I said to the student. 'I know Lilka didn't want to go anywhere. They're packing her off by force. Give me the bicycle.'

" 'Just how will you avenge me?' asked the student afraid of me. And in a few days with an innocent look I brought Lilia's aunt, as if from my mother, a remedy for warts. In a crook near her lower lip the aunt had a big wart. This aging lady covered me with kisses, her kisses giving me the impression as if I was being shot at point blank from a new sling-shot... My friends, the student was avenged. A flower grew out of the aunt's wart, a modest field bluebell. It quivered gently from the aunt's breathing. Shame fell on her head. With arms uplifted to the heavens the aunt rushed through the yard plunging everyone into panic...

"My joy was twofold. In the first place, the experiment of growing flowers out of warts was solved brilliantly, and in the second place —the student gave me the bicycle.

"And at that time, my friends, a bicycle was a rarity. Then they still drew caricatures of bicyclists."

"But what happened to the aunt?"

"Oh, my friend! She lived like that with the flower until fall. With hope she awaited the windy days and having waited it out, set out somewhere into the green surroundings, by the backways, avoiding the lively parts of the town. Moral torments tortured her. She hid her face in a scarf, the flower tickled her lips lovingly, and this tickling sounded like the whisper of despondently spent youth, like the ghost of some singular kiss almost driven out by the tramping of feet... She stopped on a hill and let down the scarf.

" 'Well, scatter, scatter it in all four directions! Well, blow, blow away its damned petals,' she prayed.

"As if out of spite the wind stopped. But in return, a mad bee flew over from the nearest summerhouse and having taken aim at the flower began to braid the poor woman with buzzing figure eights. The aunt took flight and at home, having ordered the servants not to let anyone in, sat before the mirror viewing her mythical, flower-bedecked face, which was swelling up before her eyes from a sting and turning into some sort of tropical tuber. Horror! And to simply cut the flower off—this would be too risky: there was still the wart! And suddenly blood poisoning!

Vanya Babichev was a jack-of-all-trades. He composed verses and musical pieces, drew excellently, he knew how to do most things, even made up some sort of dance designed for the employment of his external peculiarities: corpulence, indolence—he was a lout (like most remarkable people in the years of adolescence). The dance was called "The Little Jug." He sold paper snakes, whistles and lanterns; the boys envied his ability and glory. In the yard he got the nickname "Mechanic."

Besides that, Ivan Babichev finished a polytechnical institute in the mechanics division in Petersburg in exactly the year when brother Roman was executed. Ivan worked as an engineer in the town of Nikolayev near Odessa at the naval plant right until the beginning of the European war.

Then...

II

But was he ever an engineer?

In that year when "Two Bits" was being built, Ivan was occupied with a business little respected and for an engineer—simply shameful.

Imagine, in beer halls he drew portraits of those who wished, composed impromptus on given themes, determined character by the lines of a hand, demonstrated the power of his memory, repeating any five hundred words read to him without interruption.

Sometimes he took a pack of cards out of his inside pocket, instantly acquiring resemblance to a card sharp, and did tricks.

They treated him. He took a seat and then began the main event: Ivan Babichev preached.

What did he talk about?

"We—that is humanity—having reached the last limit," he said, banging a mug against the marble like a hoof. "Powerful personalities, people who've decided to live their own way, egoists, stubborn people, I turn to you as the more intelligent—my vanguard! Listen, you who are standing in the lead! An epoch is ending. The wave is breaking against the rocks, the wave bubbles, the foam sparkles. Just what do you want? What? To disappear, to come to nought like droplets, like petty water bubbling. No, my friends, you don't have to die like that! No! Come to me, I will teach you."

The listeners heeded him with some respect but with little attention, though they supported him with exclamations of "right" and at times with applause. He would disappear suddenly, each time uttering in farewell one and the same quatrain; it sounded like this:

Now I'm no German hocus-poker,
And no deceiver I of men!
I am a modest, Soviet joker,
I am the wizard back again!

And such as this was told them:

"The gates are closing. Do you hear the hissing of the sliding panels? Don't strive to pass over the threshold! Stop! Stopping is pride. Be proud. I am your leader, I am king of the vulgar. For him who sings and cries and besmirches the table with his nose when the beer's already all drunk up and they won't give him more—for him there's a place here next to me. Come, you who are heavy with grief, you who are carried by a song. You, who are killing out of jealousy or, you, who are tying your own noose—I call you both, children of the dying century: come, vulgarians and dreamers, fathers of families who cherish your daughters, honest petty bourgeois, people faithful to traditions, subjected to the norms of honor, duty, love, fearing blood and disorder, my dears—soldiers and generals—let's move out! Where to? I will lead you."

He liked to eat crayfish. Crayfish carcasses poured down under his hands. He was slovenly. His shirt, resembling a bar napkin, was always open at the chest. At the same time he also appeared, on occasion, in starched but dirty cuffs. If one could unite slovenliness with an inclination toward foppishness, then he succeded completely. For example: a derby. For example: a flower in his buttonhole (left there almost until fruition). And for example: fringe on his trousers and from several of the buttonholes of his coat only little tails.

"I am a devourer of crayfish. Look: I don't eat them, I ruin them like a priest. Do you see? Beautiful crayfish. They're enmeshed in seaweed. Ah, not seaweed? Simple greens, you say? Isn't it all the same? Let's agree that it's seaweed. That way one can compare a crayfish with a ship raised from the sea bottom. Beautiful crayfish. From the Kama."

He licked his fist and, having glanced into his cuff, extracted from it a crayfish fragment.

But was he ever an engineer? But didn't he lie? How the notion of an engineer's soul, of a closeness to machines, to metal, to blueprints, didn't square with him! One might sooner have taken him for an actor or an unfrocked priest. He himself understood that the listeners didn't believe him. He himself even spoke with some playfullness in the corner of his eye.

Now in one beer hall, now in another, appeared the plump preacher. Once he went so far that he ventured to climb up onto a table... Clumsy and in no way prepared for such feats, he climbed over heads, gripping palm leaves; bottles broke, the palm fell—he gained footing on the table and, waving two empty mugs like weights, began to shout:

"Here I stand on the heights receiving a swarming army! To me! To me! Great is my host! Little actors, dreamers of glory. Unlucky lovers! Old spinsters! Accountants! Ambitious men! Fools! Knights! Cowards! To me! Your king, Ivan Babichev, has come! The time has not yet come—soon, soon we will advance... Swarm, host!"

He flung the mug, and having snatched an accordion out of someone's hands, he unfurled it against his belly. The moan elicited by him called forth a storm; paper napkins flew up to the ceiling...

Out from behind the bar hurried people in aprons and oil cloth cuffs.

"Beer! Beer! Give us more beer! Give us a barrel of beer. We have to drink to the great events!"

But they didn't give any more beer, they threw the company out into the darkness and they drove the preacher Ivan out after them—the smallest of them, the heaviest, yielding with difficulty to ousting. Out of stubbornness and anger he suddenly acquired the weight and deathly immobility of an iron oil drum.

They pulled the derby down shamefully over his eyes.

He walked along the street staggering in all directions—just as if he were being passed from hand to hand—and plaintively half sang, half wailed, troubling the passers-by.

"Ophelia!" he sang. "Ophelia!" This one word alone; it sailed over his path, it seemed to fly over the streets quickly interlacing itself as a radiating figure eight.

That night he visited his famous brother. There were two sitting at the desk. One opposite the other. In the middle stood a lamp under a green lamp shade. Brother Andrei and Volodya were sitting. Volodya was sleeping with his head on a book. Ivan, drunk, rushed toward the sofa. He troubled himself for a long time trying to move the sofa under himself as one moves a chair.

"You're drunk, Vanya," said the brother.

"I hate you," answered Ivan. "You're an idol."

"You ought to be ashamed, Vanya! Lie down, sleep. I'll give you a pillow. Take off the derby."

"You don't believe even one of my words. You are a block-head, Andrei! Don't interrupt me. Otherwise I'll break the lamp shade over Volodya's head. Why don't you believe in the existence of 'Ophelia?' Why don't you believe that I've invented a marvelous machine?"

"You haven't invented anything, Vanya! This is an obsession with you. You play bad jokes. Now you ought to be ashamed, eh? You really take me for a fool. Now what sort of machine is it? Now could there really be such a machine? And why 'Ophelia?' And why do you wear a derby? What are you—a junkman or an ambassador?"

Ivan was silent a while. Then, as if having sobered up at once, he got up and clenching his fists went at his brother:

"You don't believe? You don't believe? Andrei, stand up when the leader of an army of many millions is talking to you. You dare not to believe me? You say there is no such machine? Andrei, I promise you: you'll die from this machine."

"Don't make a row," the brother answered, "you'll wake Volodya."

"Spit on your Volodya. I know, I know your plans. You want to give my daughter to Volodya. You want to raise a new breed. My daughter is not an incubator. You won't get her. I won't give her to Volodya. I'll strangle her with my very own hands."

He made a pause and with playfulness in the corner of his eye, thrusting his hands into his pockets and as if lifting his bulging-out paunch with his hands, said in a tone full of malice:

"You're making a mistake, little brother. You're throwing dust into your own eyes. Ho-ho, dear heart. You think that you love Volodya because Volodya's a new man? Not a chance, Andrusha, not a chance... It's not that, Andrusha, it's not that... It's something else entirely."

"Just what?" Andrei asked threateningly.

"You're simply getting old, Andrusha! And you simply need a son. And you're simply experiencing fatherly feelings. The family— it's eternal, Andrei! And symbolization of the new world in the form of a scarcely remarkable youth well-known only on the soccer field— that's nonsense..."

Volodya raised his head.

"Greetings to the Edison of the new century!" exclaimed Ivan. "Hurrah!" and bowed magnificently.

Volodya looked at him silently. Ivan guffawed.

"How about it, Edison? Don't you believe that there's such an 'Ophelia' either?"

"You, Ivan Petrovich, should be put into a Kanatchikov summer home," said Volodya yawning.

Andrei emitted a short neigh.

Then the preacher flung his derby on the floor.

"Boors!" he shouted. And after a pause: "Andrei! Do you allow it? Why do you allow a foundling to insult your brother?"

Here Ivan didn't see his brother's eyes—Ivan saw only the sparkle of the lenses.

"Ivan," said Andrei. "I beg you never to come here. You're not a madman. You're a beast."

III

Conversations went on about the new preacher.

From the beer halls the rumor spread to apartments, crept along service entrances into communal kitchens—at the hour of morning ablutions, at the hour of the igniting of hot plates, people keeping an eye on milk which was about to run over and others dancing under the shower-head wore out the gossip.

The rumor penetrated into offices, rest homes and markets.

A story was composed about how an unknown citizen came to a bank collector's for a wedding, at Yakimanka (in a derby, the details were pointed out, a shabby, suspicious person—none other than he, Babichev, Ivan) and having appeared before everyone at the very height of the feast, demanded attention in order to make a speech—an address to the newlyweds. He said:

"You don't have to love one another. There's no need to be united. Bridegroom, forsake the bride! What sort of fruit will your love bring you? You'll bring your own enemy into the world. He'll devour you."

The bridegroom apparently was spoiling for a fight. The bride dropped to the ground. The guest retreated in great offense and it was apparently discovered at once that the port in all the bottles standing on the festal table had turned into water.

Still another marvelous story was thought up.

Passing apparently through a very noisy place (some named Neglinny by Kuznetsky Bridge, others—Tverskaya by Passion Monastery) was an automobile in which sat a solid citizen, stout, red-cheeked, with a briefcase on his knees.

And apparently out of a crowd form the sidewalk ran his brother Ivan, that very same famous person. Having seen his brother riding along, he took a stand in the path of the car, throwing open his arms as a scarecrow stands or as, threatening, one stops a stampeding horse. The chauffeur managed to reduce speed. He beeped the horn, continuing to ride on, but the scarecrow didn't get off the road.

"Stop!" exclaimed the man at the top of his voice. "Stop, commissar. Stop, abductor of another's children!"

And there was nothing left for the chauffeur but to apply the brakes. The flow of traffic stopped short. Many cars almost reared up flying onto the one in front and, having roared, a bus stopped, getting all uneasy, ready to submit, to raise its elephantine tires and to backtrack...

The outstretched arms of the one standing on the pavement demanded silence.

And everything fell silent.

"Brother," uttered the man. "Why do you ride in a car while I walk? Open the door, move aside, let me in. Walking doesn't suit me either. You're a leader, but I'm a leader too."

And indeed, at these words people ran up to him from various directions, some jumped out of the bus, others abandoned the local beer halls, a third group rushed up from the boulevard—and that brother sitting in the automobile, getting up, huge, having increased in size due to the automobile's standing still, saw before himself a living barricade.

His threatening look was such that it seemed he would immediately step out and go over the car, over the chauffeur's back onto them, onto the barricade, smashing—against the whole length of the street—like a pillar.

And Ivan—they just lifted onto their hands: he rose over the crowd of his followers, rocked, fell through, pulled himself up; his derby dropped to the back of his head and uncovered was the large, serene forehead of a tired man.

And brother Andrei pulled him down from the height, grabbing his pants at the stomach with a squeeze. And thus he flung him to a policeman.

"To the G. P. U!" he said.

Hardly had the magic word been pronounced when everything came out of its lethargy, rousing itself: spokes sparkled, bushings whirled, doors slammed and all those actions which were begun before the lethargy got their further development.

Ivan was under arrest for ten days.

When they returned his freedom to him, his drinking buddies asked him if it was true that he was arrested on the street by his brother under such astonishing circumstances. He guffawed.

"That's a lie. A legend. They simply arrested me in a beer hall. I suppose that there's been observation of me for a long time already. But all the same it's good that legends are already being made up. The end of an epoch, a time of transition, needs its legends and tales. After all, I'm fortunate that I'll be the hero of one such tale. And there will be one more legend: about a machine that carried the name 'Ophelia'... The epoch will die with my name on its lips. I'm directing my efforts towards just that."

They let him out, threatening him with exile.

With what could they have incriminated him in the G. P. U?

"Did you call yourself king?" asked the investigator.

"Yes...king of the vulgar."

"What does that mean?"

"You see, I'm opening the eyes of a large category of people..."

"To what are you opening their eyes?"

"They have to understand their predestination."

"You said: a large category of people. Whom do you mean by this category?"

"All those whom you call decadents. Bearers of the decadent mood. Allow me, I'll explain in detail."

"I'll be obliged to you."

"...a whole series of human feelings seems to me to be destined for destruction..."

"For example? The feelings..."

"...of pity, tenderness, pride, jealousy, love—in a word, almost all the feelings of which is composed the soul of the man of the ending era. The era of socialism will create in place of the former sensations a new series of states of the human soul."

"That's right."

"I see you don't understand me. The communist bitten by the snake of jealousy is subject to persecutions. And the compassionate communist is also subject to persecutions. The buttercup of pity, the lizard of vanity, the snake of jealousy—this flora and fauna has to be driven out of the heart of the new man.

"...You'll excuse me, I'm speaking a little colorfully, does it seem flowery to you? It's not difficult for you? I thank you. Water? No, I don't want any water... I love to speak beautifully...

"...we know that the grave of a young communist who dies by his own hand is adorned alternately with wreaths as well as the curses of his comrades. The man of the new world says: suicide is a decadent act. But the man of the old world says: he had to take his own life in order to save his honor. By this we see that the new man is schooling himself to despise the ancient feelings glorified by the poets and the very muse of history. Well, there you are. I want to arrange the last parade of these feelings."

"And this is what you call the conspiracy of feelings?"

"Yes. This is the conspiracy of feelings at the head of which I stand."

"Continue."

"Yes. I would like to unite around myself a certain troup. Do you understand?

"...you see, one must admit that the old feelings were beautiful. Instances of great love, let's say, for a woman or for the fatherland. All sorts of things! You must admit that something from these memories still stirs even now. It's true, isn't it? And so I'd like...

"...you know, it happens that an electric bulb will unexpectedly go out. It burned out, you say. And if you shake this burned out bulb then it'll light up again and will still burn for some time. Inside the bulb a catastrophe is taking place. Tungsten filaments break off and through the contact of the fragments life returns to the bulb. A short, unnatural, undisguisedly doomed life—a fever, an overly bright incandescence, a brilliance. Then will come the darkness, life will not return, and in the darkness the dead scorched filaments will only rattle. Do you understand? But the brief brilliance is beautiful.

"...I want to shake...

"...I want to shake the heart of the burned out epoch. The heart-bulb, so that the fragments would touch.

"...and to bring about a momentary, beautiful brilliance.

"...and I want to find representatives from there, from what you call the old world. I have in mind those feelings: jealousy, love for a woman, honesty. I want to find a real dolt in order to show you: here, comrades, is a representative of that human state which is called 'stupidity.'

"...many characters played out the comedy of the old world. The curtain is closing. The personages must gather at the proscenium to say the last couplets. I want to be a mediator between them and the audience. I will conduct the chorus and will leave the stage last.

"...to me has fallen the honor of leading the old human passions in the last parade...

"...through the eye-slits of a mask history follows us with a twinkling gaze. And I want to show her: here's a man in love, here's an ambitious man, here's a traitor, here's a recklessly brave man, here's a true friend, here's a prodigal son—here they are, bearers of the great feelings now labeled as insignificant and vulgar. Let them for the last time before they disappear, before they undergo derision, let them be manifest in high tension.

"...I listen to the conversation of others. They're talking about a razor. About a madman who had slit his throat. Here a woman's name pops us. He didn't die, the madman, they sewed up his throat—and again he slashed it along the same place. Who is he? Point him out, I need him, I'm looking for him. And I'm looking for her too. For her, the demonic woman, and for him, the tragic lover. But where should one look for him? In Sklifosovsky Hospital? And her? Who's she? An office girl? A Nep-girl?"

"...it's very difficult for me to find heroes...

"...there are no heroes...

"...I peep into other people's windows, go up other people's staircases. At times I run after someone else's smile, skipping as a naturalist running after a butterfly! I feel like shouting: 'Stop! With what blooms the bush from which flew out the delicate and precipitant butterfly of your smile? This is the bush of what feeling? The pink sweetbrier of melancholy or the black currant of petty vanity? Stop! I need you'...

"...I want to gather a multitude around myself. In order to have a choice and to choose the best, the most striking of them, to make a sort of shock group...a group of feelings.

"...yes, this is a conspiracy, a peaceful uprising. A peaceful demonstration of feelings.

"...let's say that somewhere I hunt up a full-blooded, one-hundred-percent ambitious man. I'll say to him: 'Show yourself! Show those who don't give you a chance, show them what ambition is perform an act about which they'll say: "Oh, base ambition! oh, such is the force of ambition".' Or let's say, I'll be lucky enough to find an ideal lightminded man. And I'll ask him too: 'Show yourself, show the force of lightmindedness so the audience will throw up its hands!'

"...the genii of feelings rule souls. The genie of pride drives one soul, another soul the genie of compassion. I want to evoke them, these devils, and let them out into the arena."

Investigator. Well then, have you already managed to find someone?

Ivan. For a long time I've been calling, for a long time I've been searching. It's very difficult. Perhaps they don't understand me. But I have found one.

Investigator. Who, exactly?

Ivan. Are you interested in the feeling of which he's the bearer, or his name?

Investigator. Both.

Ivan. Nikolai Kavalerov. Envier.

IV

They stepped away from the mirror.

Now the two comics were walking together. One, shorter and stouter, passed ahead of the other by a step. This was a peculiarity of Ivan Babichev. Conversing with his companion he was forced constantly to look around. If he had to pronounce a long sentence (and his sentences were never short) then more than once, walking with his face turned toward his companion, he would run into passers-by. Then he would immediately take off his derby and break into pompous apologies. He was a courteous person. The welcoming smile didn't leave his face.

The day closed shop. A gypsy in a blue vest with painted cheeks and a beard carried lifted up on his shoulder a clean, copper basin. The day moved away on the shoulder of the gypsy. The disc of the basin was bright and blind. The gypsy walked slowly, the basin rocked lightly and the day turned in the disc.

The wayfarers followed with their eyes.

And the disc set like the sun. The day ended.

The wayfarers at once turned into a beer hall.

Kavalerov told Ivan about how an important person had kicked him out of his house. He didn't give his name. Ivan told him the same sort of thing: an important person had driven him out too.

"And you probably know him. Everyone knows him. It's my brother, Andrei Petrovich Babichev. Heard of him?"

Turning red, Kavalerov lowered his eyes. He didn't give any answer.

"In this our fate is similar and we must be friends," said Ivan beaming. "And I like the name Kavalerov: it's pompous and base."

Kavalerov thought: "I am pompous and base."

"Excellent beer!" exclaimed Ivan. "The Poles say: she has beer-colored eyes. Isn't that good?"

"...But the main thing is that this famous person, my brother, stole my daughter from me...

"...I'll take revenge on my brother...

"...He stole my daughter from me. Well, he didn't literally steal her of course... Don't make big eyes, Kavalerov. And it wouldn't hurt you to make your nose smaller. With a fat nose you have to be famous like a hero in order to be happy like a simple Philistine. He exerted moral influence over her. Could one be tried for that? Brought to the public prosecutor, eh? She left me. I don't even blame Andrei so much as that swine that's living with him."

He told about Volodya.

On Kavalerov's feet the big toes stirred from embarrassment.

"...This little boy ruined my life. Oh, if only he'd get the kidneys knocked out of him at soccer. Andrei listens to him about everything. He, that little boy, you see, is the new man. The little boy said that Valya was unhappy because I, the father, was a madman and that

[74]

I (the swine) was systematically driving her out of her mind. Swine! Together they persuaded her. And Valya ran away. Some girl-friend took her in.

"...I cursed this girl-friend. I wished that her esophagus and her rectum would change place. Get the picture? They're a bunch of hard heads...

"...woman was the best, the most beautiful, the purest flower of our culture. I looked for a being of the female sex. I looked for the sort of being in whom all feminine qualities would be united. I looked for the ovary of feminine qualities. Femininity was the glory of the old age. I wanted to make a brilliant display of this femininity. We are dying, Kavalerov. I wanted to carry woman over my head like a torch. I thought that woman would die out along with our era. Milleniums stand like a sewer hole. In the hole wallow machines, pieces of cast iron, of tin, screws, springs... A dark, gloomy hole. And in the hole shine pieces of rotten wood, phosphorescent fungi—mould. These are our feelings! This is all that is left of our feelings, of the flowering of our souls. The new man comes to the hole, rummages, climbs into it, chooses what he needs—some part of machine proves useful, a little nut—and the pieces of rotten wood he tramples, extinguishes. I dreamed of finding a woman who would blossom in this hole with unprecedented feeling. Like the wonderful flowering of a fern. So that the new man coming to steal our iron would be frightened, would jerk back his hand, close his eyes blinded by the light of what to him seemed a piece of rotten wood.

"...I found such a being. Right beside me. Valya. I thought that Valya would shine over the dying age, light its way to the great cemetery. But I was mistaken. She flitted away. She left the bedside of the old age. I thought that woman was ours, that tenderness and love were only ours—but there...I was mistaken. And so, the last dreamer on earth, I wander along the edge of the hole like a wounded bat..."

Kavalerov thought: "I'll snatch Valya from them." He felt like telling that he was a witness to the incident on the side street where the hedge bloomed. But for some reason he refrained.

"Our fates our similar," continued Ivan. "Give me your hand. That's it. I welcome you. Very glad to see you, young man. Let's clink glasses. So they drove you out, Kavalerov? Tell me about it, tell me. However, you've already told me. A very important person turned you out? You don't want to name names? Well, all right. You hate this man very much?"

Kavalerov nods.

"Oh, how understandable it all is to me, my boy. You, as far as I understand you, snubbed a powerful man. Don't interrupt me. You came to hate a man recognized by everyone. It seems to you, of course, that it was he who offended you. Don't interrupt me. Drink.

"...you're convinced that it's he who's preventing you from proving yourself, that he's seized your rights, that there, where it's necessary in your opinion for you to dominate, he dominates. And you're furious..."

The orchestra soars in the smoke. The pale face of the violinist is lying on the violin.

"The violin resembles the violinist himself," says Ivan. "It's a small violinist in a wooden tailcoat. Do you hear? The wood is singing. Do you hear the voice of the wood? The wood in the orchestra sings with various voices. But how badly they're playing! God, how badly they're playing."

He turned around to the musicians.

"You think you have a drum? You think the drum is playing its part? No, it's the god of music knocking on you with his fist.

"...my friend, envy is gnawing at us. We envy the approaching epoch. If you wish, here is the envy of old age. Here is the envy of the first human generation to have grown old. Let's talk about envy. Give us some more beer..."

They sat by a wide window.

Once again it had rained. It was evening. The city sparkled as if carved from Cardiff coal: pressing their noses, people peeped in the window from Samotyoka.

"...yes, envy. Here a drama has to be performed, one of those grandiose dramas in the theater of history which for a long time evoke the crying, the raptures, the regrets and the anger of humanity. You, without realizing it yourself, are the bearer of a historic mission. You, so to say, are a clot. You are a clot of the envy of the dying epoch. The dying epoch envies what is coming in its place."

"What can I do?" asked Kavalerov.

"My dear boy, here you have to reconcile yourself or...make a scandal. Or you have to leave with a bang. Slam the door as they say. There's the main thing: to leave with a bang. So that a scar remains on the mug of history—show off, devil take you! They won't let you in there anyway. Don't give in without a fight...I want to tell you about one incident from my childhood...

"...a ball was arranged. The children put on a play, performed a ballet on a specially-set-up stage in the large parlor. And a little girl—can you picture it?—such a typical little girl, twelve years old, slender-legged, in a short little dress, all pink, satiny, all dolled up— well, you know, on the whole, with her little frills, bows, resembling the flower known by the name 'snapdragon': a little beauty, haughty, spoiled, shaking her locks—just such a little girl set the step at that ball. She was the queen. She did whatever she wanted, everyone admired her, everything emanated from her, everything drew towards her. She danced, sang, jumped and thought up games better than everyone else. The best gifts fell to her, the best candies, flowers, oranges, praises... I was thirteen, I was a gymansium student. She didn't give me a chance. Whereas I, too, had become accustomed to rapture, I, too, was spoiled by worship. In my classroom I was even dominant, was the record holder. I couldn't stand it. I caught the little girl in the corridor and gave her a thrashing, tore off her ribbons, let down her locks into the wind, scratched up her charming physiognomy. I grabbed her by the back of the head and knocked her forehead against a column several times. At that moment I loved this girl more than life, worshipped her—and hated her with all my might. Tearing the beauty's curls I thought that I'd shame her, disperse her pinkness, her brilliance, and thought that I'd correct the mistake made by everyone. But nothing came of it. The shame fell on me. I was driven out. However, my dear boy, they remembered me all evening; however, I did spoil the ball for them; however, they did talk about me everywhere the beauty appeared... Thus, I experienced envy for the first time. The heartburn of envy is horrible. How oppressive it is to envy! Envy squeezes the throat with a spasm, squeezes the eyes out of their orbits. When I was tormenting her there in the corridor, the captured victim, tears were rolling from my eyes, I was choking—and nevertheless I tore her ravishing clothes, shuddering from the contact with the satin—it evoked almost a soreness on my teeth and lips. You know what satin's like, the nap of satin—you know how contact with it runs through the spine, the whole nervous system, what sort of grimaces it evokes! So all forces rose up against me in defense of the nasty girl. Soreness, poison, concealed in the bushes and baskets, flowed out from that which had seemed so charmingly innocent in the parlor—out of her dress, out of the pink satin so sweet to the eyes. I don't remember whether I emitted any cries while committing my reprisal. I probably whispered: 'Here's revenge for you! Don't crowd me. Don't take away what might belong to me'...

"...Did you listen to me carefully? I want to make a certain analogy. I have in mind the battle of the epochs. Of course, at first glance the comparison will seem frivolous. But do you understand me? I'm talking about envy."

The orchestra members finished the number.

"Well, thank God," said Ivan. "They've stopped. Look: a cello. It sparkled much less before they took it up. They tormented it for a long time. Now it sparkles like it's wet, really a refreshed cello. You have to jot down my judgments, Kavalerov. I don't talk—I carve my words in marble. Isn't that true?..

"...My dear boy, we were record holders, we too are spoiled by worship, we too got accustomed to dominating there...in our place... Where is our place?... There, in the waning epoch. Oh, how beautiful the rising world! Oh, how the holiday luminesces there—where they won't let us in! Everything emanates from it, from the new epoch, everything draws toward it, it will receive the best gifts and raptures. I love it, this world, impending on me, more than life, I admire it and hate it with all my might! I'm choking, tears are rolling from my eyes like rain, but I want to thrust my fingers into its clothes, to tear. Don't crowd me! Don't take away what might belong to me...

"...We must get revenge. Both you and I—there are many thousands of us—we must get revenge. Kavalerov, not always do enemies turn out to be windmills. Sometimes what we would like to take for a windmill is an enemy, an aggressor bearing destruction and death. Your enemy, Kavalerov, is a real enemy. Take vengeance on him.

Believe me, we'll take the young world down a peg. We aren't sewn of bast either. We too were pets of history.

"...Force yourself to talk about yourself. It's clear: everything's going to destruction, everything's planned out, there's no way out— you're to perish, fat nose! Every minute will increase the humiliation, with every day the enemy will blossom like a cherished youth. To perish: it's clear. So embellish your destruction, decorate it with fireworks, tear the clothes off him who's crowding you, bid farewell in such a way that your 'good-bye' will roll on through the ages."

Kavalerov thought: "He's reading my thoughts."

"Did they offend you? Did they drive you out?"

"They offended me frightfully," Kavalerov said hotly, "they humiliated me for a long time."

"Who offended you? One of the chosen of the epoch?"

"Your brother," Kavalerov wanted to shout, "the same one who offended you." But he remained silent.

"You're lucky. You don't know the aggressor on sight. You have a concrete enemy. And so do I."

"What should I do?"

"You're lucky. You can unite the atonement for yourself with the atonement for the epoch which was a mother to you."

"What should I do?"

"Kill him. Respectfully leave a remembrance of yourself as the hired assassin of the age. Smash your enemy on the threshold of two epochs. He's pluming himself, he's already there, he's already a genie, a cupid hovering with a scroll at the gates of the new world, lifting his nose he no longer sees us—belt him in farewell. I bless you. And I (Ivan raised his mug) and I, too, will destroy my enemy. Let's drink, Kavalerov, to 'Ophelia'. That's the instrument of my vengeance."

Kavalerov opened his mouth to report the main thing: we have a common enemy, you blessed me for the murder of your brother— but he didn't say a word, because a man came up to their table asking Ivan to follow him at once and without asking any questions. He was arrested, of which is known from the preceding chapter.

"Good-bye, my dear boy," said Ivan, "they're taking me to Golgotha. Go to my daughter (he named the sidestreet already long ago blazing in Kavalerov's memory), go and look at her. You'll understand that if such a creation betrayed us, then only one thing is left: vengeance.

He drank up his beer and walked away one step ahead of the mysterious man.

On the way he winked at the customers, poured out smiles, glanced in the bell of the clarinet and right at the door turned around, and holding his derby in his outstretched hand, declaimed:

> Now I'm no German hocus-poker,
> And no deceiver I of men!
> I am a modest, Soviet joker,
> I am the wizard back again!

V

"Why are you laughing? Do you think I want to sleep?" asked Volodya.

"But I'm not laughing. I'm coughing."

And reaching the chair Volodya again fell asleep.

The young one got tired earlier. That one, the older—Andrei Babichev—was a giant. He worked the day, worked half the night. Andrei banged on the desk with his fist. The lamp shade on the lamp jumped up like the cover on a teapot but that one slept. The lamp shade jumped. Andrei remembered James Watt looking at the cover of a teapot jumping over the steam.

A well-known legend. A well-known picture.

James Watt invented the steam engine.

"What are you inventing, my James Watt? What kind of machine are you inventing, Volodya? What new secret of nature will you uncover, new man?"

And here began a conversation of Andrei Babichev with himself. For a very short time he dropped his work and, looking at the one who was sleeping, thought:

"But perhaps Ivan is right? Perhaps I'm simply an ordinary

Philistine and domesticity dwells in me? Is he dear to me because he's been living with me since childhood years, because I've simply become accustomed to him, grown fond of him like a son? Is it only for that? Is it that simple? And if he was a dolt? That for the sake of which I live, focused in him. I lucked out. The life of the new humanity is far away. I believe in it. And I lucked out. Here he's fallen asleep so close to me, my beautiful new world. The new world lives in my house. I don't dote on him. A son? A foothold? Someone to close my eyelids? Not true! That's not what I need! I don't want to die on high bedding, on pillows. I know: a mass and not a family will take in my last breath. Nonsense! As we cherish that new world, so I cherish him. And he's dear to me as personified hope. I'll chase him out, if I'm deceived in him, if he's not new, not completely different from me because I'm still standing up to my belly in the old and now I won't get out. I'll chase him out then: I don't need a son, I'm not a father and he's not a son, we aren't a family. I'm the one who believed in him and he's the one who warranted belief.

"We aren't a family, we are humanity.

"What does it mean? Does it mean the human feeling of fatherly love has to be destroyed? Why does he love me, he, the new? Does it mean that there too, in the new world, love will blossom between son and father? Then I get the right to rejoice; then I'm in the right to love him both as a son and as a new man. Ivan, Ivan, your conspiracy is worthless. Not all feelings will perish. You're furious for nothing, Ivan!"

Long, long ago on a dark night, falling into ravines, up to their knees in stars, scaring the stars from the bushes, two people were fleeing: a commissar and a boy. The boy saved the commissar. The commissar was huge, the boy—a crumb. Anyone seeing them would have thought: running alone—a giant falling to the ground, and the boy they would have taken for the giant's palm.

They were united forever.

The boy lived with the giant, grew, grew up, became a Young Communist and became a student. He was born in a railroad workers' settlement, was the son of a foundry repairman.

His comrades loved him, adults loved him. It never disturbed him that everyone liked him—this at times seemed to him undeserved and mistaken. The feeling of comradeship was in him the very strongest. As if caring about some sort of equilibrium and trying to correct some sort of irregularity allowed by nature in the distribution of talents, he sometimes resorted even to contrivances with the aim of smoothing over the impression of himself, lowering it, and hurried to extinguish his own luster.

He felt like compensating the less successful of his age group by his devotion, by self-sacrifice, by an ardent display of friendship, by finding in each of them remarkable traits and abilities. His companionship incited his comrades to competition.

"I was thinking why people feel angry or feel offended," he said. "Such people don't have an understanding of time. Here there's an ignorance of technology. Time is really also a technical understanding. If everyone were a technician, then spite, self-esteem and all petty feeling would disappear. You're smiling? You understand: it's necessary to understand time in order to get far from petty feelings. An offense, let's say, lasts an hour or a year. They have enough imagination for a year. But for a thousand years they won't gather momentum. They see only three or four divisions on the dial, they crawl, fuss... It's out of their reach! They won't embrace the whole dial. And in general: tell them that there is a dial—they won't believe it."

"So why only the petty feelings then? The lofty feelings are brief too, aren't they? Well... magnanimity?"

"You see now. You just listen to me. In magnanimity there's some sort of regularity—technical. Don't you smile. Yes, yes. No, as a matter of fact...I seem to have gotten mixed up. You confuse me. No, wait! The revolution was...well, what? Of course, very cruel. Ho! But for the sake of what was it malicious? It was magnanimous, right? Was good—for the whole dial...Right! One has to take offense not in the space between two divisions but in the whole circle of the dial... Then there is no difference between cruelty and magnanimity. Then there is only one:time. The iron, as it's said, logic of history. And history and time are one and the same, doubles. Don't laugh, Andrei Petrovich. I say: the main feeling of man must be the understanding of time."

He said also:

"I'll knock the bourgeois world down a few pegs. They're

jeering at us. The old men grumble: where are your new engineers, surgeons, professors, inventors? I'll father a big group of comrades, about a hundred men. We'll organize a union. For the knocking down of the bourgeois world a few pegs. You think I'm bragging? You don't understand anything. I'm not getting carried away at all. We will work like beasts. You'll see. They'll come to us to bow down. And Valya will be in this union."

He woke up.

"I had a dream," he began to laugh, "apparently Valya and I are sitting on a roof and looking into a telescope at the moon."

"What? Uh? A telescope?"

"And I'm saying to her: 'Over there, down below, the Sea of Crises.' And she asks: 'Sea of Mice?' "

That year in the spring Volodya left for a short period to see his father in the town of Murom. The father worked in the Murom locomotive construction shops. Two days of separation passed and on the night of the third day Andrei was riding home. At a turn the chauffeur reduced speed, it was getting light and Andrei saw a man lying by a wall.

A reminder of the one who was absent flew to him from the one who was lying on the grating. It ordered him to be pulled and to be bent toward the chauffeur. "But there's nothing in common between them," Andrei nearly exclaimed. And really there was no resemblance between the one lying and the one absent. He simply pictured Volodya to himself vividly. He thought: "And suddenly something forced Volodya to take such a pitiful pose." And he simply did a stupid thing, let sentimentality run high! The car stopped.

Nikolai Kavalerov was lifted up, his delirious words were listened to.

Andrei brought him home, dragged him up to the third floor and laid him on Volodya's sofa, arranged bedding for him and covered him up to his neck with a rug; that one lay flat on his back with the waffle-like print of the grating on his cheek. The host went off to sleep in good humor: the sofa was not standing empty.

That same night he dreamed that a young man hanged himself on a telescope.

VI

In Annechka Prokopovich's room stood a remarkable bed—of expensive wood covered with dark cherry varnish, with mirror arches on the inward side of the back-board.

Once, in a profoundly peaceful year, at a folk fair, to the sound of fanfares, sprinkled with confetti, Annechka's husband went up onto a wooden stand and having produced a lottery ticket, received from the manager a receipt for the right of possession over the remarkable bed. They carried it off by means of a cart. Small boys whistled.

The azure sky was reflected in the moving mirror arches, just as though the lids of beautiful eyes were opening and slowly closing.

The family lived, fell to pieces—the bed passed through all adversities.

Kavalerov lives in the corner behind the bed.

He came to Annechka and said:

"I can pay you thirty rubles a month for the corner."

Smiling broadly, Annechka agreed.

He had nowhere to go. A new tenant had settled firmly in his former room. Kavalerov had sold the frightful bed for four rubles, and it left him with moans.

Annechka's bed resembled an organ. Half the room was occupied by it. Its height melted in the dusk of the ceiling.

Kavalerov was thinking:

"If I were a child, Annechka's little son—how many poetic, enchanted constructions my childish mind would create given over to the power of the sight of such an unusual thing. Now I'm grown up and now I catch only the general contours and only certain of the details, but then I would have been able to....

...But then submitting neither to distances, nor to scales, nor to time, nor to weight, nor to gravity, I would have crawled in the corridors formed by the void between the frame of the spring mattress and the sides of the bed; I would have hidden behind the columns which now seem to me no bigger than graduates; I would have set up imaginary catapults on its barricades and shot at the enemy losing force in flight along the soft, engulfing ground of the blanket; I would have arranged receptions of ambassadors under the mirror arches like the king in the novel I'd just read; I would have set out on fantastic journeys along the fretwork ever higher and higher— along the legs and buttocks of cupids, would have crawled over them as they crawl over a statue of Buddha not knowing how to embrace it with a glance, and from the last arch, from the dizzying height I would have fallen into the frightful gulf, into the icy gulf of pillows...."

Ivan Babichev leads Kavalerov along a green bank.... Dandelions fly out from under their feet, float—their floating is a dynamic reflection of the intense heat.... From the intense heat Babichev pales. His full face sparkles, the intense heat just sculptures a mask out of his face.

"Over here!" he commands.

The suburb is blooming.

They cross a vacant lot, go along fences; sheep dogs rage behind the fences, clank their chains. Kavalerov whistles, teasing the sheep dogs—but anything is possible: suddenly one of them will slip loose, break the chain and jump over the fence—and therefore a capsule of terror dissolves somewhere in the pit of the teaser's stomach.

The wayfarers descend along a green slope almost onto the roofs of little red houses, onto the tops of gardens. The district is unfamiliar to Kavalerov and even seeing before him the Krestovsky towers he is unable to orient himself. Whistles of locomotives are heard, railroad clang.

"I'll show you my machine," Ivan said looking back at Kavalerov. "Pinch yourself...that's it...again...and again.... It's not a dream? No? Remember: everything was simple, you and I went across a vacant lot, a puddle that never dries up was sparkling, pots were put up on the palings; remember, my friend, it was possible to note remarkable things in the trash, under the fences in the ditches: for example, look—a page from a book—bend down, look, before the wind carries it away—you see: illustrations to *Taras Bulba,* recognize them? It must be that they threw the wrapper from something edible out of that little window there and the page fell here. Further—what's this. The eternal traditional shoe in a ditch? It's not worth paying attention to it—it's too academic an image of desolation. Further—a bottle...wait, it's still whole, but tomorrow the wheel of a cart will crush it, and if soon after us some other sort of dreamer passes along our path, he will receive full enjoyment from the contemplation of the famous bottle glass, of the famous fragment glorified by writers for its ability to suddenly flash up amidst trash and desolation and to create all sorts of mirages for lonely travelers.... Observe, my friend, observe.... Here are buttons, hoops, here's a shred of bandage, here are the Babylonian towers of petrified, human defecation.... In a word, my friend—the usual relief of a vacant lot.... Remember. Everything was simple. And I was leading you to show you my machine. Pinch yourself. That's it. Then, it's not a dream? Well, all right. But then afterwards—I know what will be afterwards—you'll say that you didn't feel well, that it was too hot, that, possibly, a lot of it seemed that way to you because of the heat, fatigue and so on. No, my friend, I demand that you confirm that you find yourself in the most normal state. That which you will now see may stun you too strongly."

Kavalerov confirmed:

"I find myself in the most normal state."

And there was a fence, a little, low plank fence.

"It's there," said Ivan. "Wait. Let's sit down. Over here, over the little ravine. I tell you: my dream was the machine of machines, the universal machine. I thought about the perfect instrument, I hoped to concentrate hundreds of different functions in one small apparatus. Yes, my friend. A beautiful, noble task. For the sake of this it was worth becoming a fanatic. I had the thought of subduing the mastodon of technology, to make him tame, domestic.... To give man such a little lever, simple, familiar, which wouldn't frighten him, would be ordinary, like a doorknob...."

"I don't understand anything about mechanics," uttered Kavalerov, "I'm afraid of machines...."

"And I succeeded. Listen to me, Kavalerov. I invented such a machine."

(The fence beckoned and, however, it was most likely assumed that there was no secret behind the usual, gray boards.)

"It can blow up mountains. It can fly. It lifts weights. It crushes ore. It replaces the kitchen range, the baby carriage, the long-range weapon.... It's the genie of mechanics itself...."

"Why are you smiling, Ivan Petrovich?"

(Ivan had playfulness in the corner of his eye.)

"I'm blooming. I can't talk about it without my heart jumping like an egg in boiling water. Listen to me. I endowed it with a hundred skills. I invented a machine which can do everything. Do you understand me? You'll see it right away, but...."

He stood up and, having placed his palm on Kavalerov's shoulder, said solemnly:

"But I've prohibited it. One fine day I understood that it is to me that the supernatural possibility of getting revenge for my epoch has been given.... I've corrupted the machine. On purpose. Out of spite."

He burst out laughing in a happy laugh.

"No, understand, Kavalerov, what great satisfaction. I endowed the greatest creation of technology with the most vulgar human feelings! I disgraced the machine. I got revenge for my age, which gave me the brain that lies in my skull, my brain which thought up the marvelous machine.... Whom to leave it to? To the new world? They're devouring us like food—they're drawing the nineteenth century into themselves like a boa constrictor draws in a rabbit.... They chew and digest. What's of use—they imbibe, what's injurious— they throw away.... Our feelings they throw away, our technology— imbibe. They won't get my machine, won't use me, won't imbibe my brain.... My machine could make the new age happy, at once from the first days could bring technology into bloom. But there— they won't get it. The machine is mine—it's a blinding fig which the dying age will show to the one being born. Their mouths will water when they see it. The machine—just think—their idol, the machine.... and suddenly.... And suddenly the best of machines turns out to be a liar, a vulgarian, a sentimental scoundrel! Let's go...I'll show you.... That which can do everything—it sings our love songs now, stupid love songs of the old age, and gathers the flowers of the old age. It falls in love, is jealous, cries, has dreams.... I did this. I made a

laughing stock out of the deity of these people to come, of the
machine. And I gave it the name of a girl gone out of her mind from
love and despair—the name of Ophelia.... The most human, most
touching...."

Ivan drew Kavalerov after him.

Ivan pressed close to a chink, exposing to Kavalerov a glossy,
brazen rear—just like dumbbells. Perhaps the heat, the unusual, remote
emptiness, the novelty of a landscape unexpected for Moscow did have
an influence, perhaps fatigue really did have an effect, but only Kavalerov, left alone in the desertedness and remoteness from legalized
city noises, gave way to some mirage, some auditory hallucination.
As if the voice of Ivan was heard conversing with someone through
the chink. Then Ivan recoiled. And Kavalerov did the same, although
he was standing at a considerable distance from Ivan—as if fright were
hiding somewhere in the trees opposite or held them both on one
thread which it had pulled.

"Who's whistling?" shouted Kavalerov in a voice ringing from
fear.

A piercing whistle flew over the neighborhood. Kavalerov turned
away for an instant hiding his face with his palms, as you turn away in
a draft. Ivan ran from the fence at Kavalerov—as if sowing his short steps
—the whistle flew after him, as if Ivan wasn't running but sliding, strung
on the blinding ray of the whistle.

"I'm afraid of her! I'm afraid of her!" Kavalerov heard the pant-
ing whisper of Ivan.

Having gripped hands, they ran downward accompanied by the
curses of an alarmed tramp whom at first from the height they had
taken for an old harness thrown away by someone....

The tramp, torn out of sleep in a swoop, sat on a hummock
rummaging in the grass—he was looking for a rock. They stole into a
lane.

"I'm afraid of her," Ivan said quickly. "She hates me.... She's
betrayed me.... She'll kill me..."

Kavalerov, coming to, was ashamed of his cowardice. He remembered that then, when he'd seen Ivan taking flight, still something else
appeared to his vision which, being frightened, he didn't have time to
register.

"Listen," he said, "what nonsense! A boy just whistled through his fingers. I saw. A boy appeared on the fence and whistled. Well yes, a boy...."

"I said to you," Ivan smiled, "I said that you'd begin to look for all sorts of explanations. I begged you: pinch yourself harder."

A quarrel took place. Ivan turned into a beer hall found with difficulty. He didn't invite Kavalerov. That one plodded along, not knowing the way, seeking the trolley ring with his ear. But on the nearest corner, stomping his foot, Kavalerov turned into the beer hall. Ivan met him with a smile and a palm directed toward a chair.

"Now tell me," implored Kavalerov. "Now answer me, why are you tormenting me? Why are you deceiving us? There really isn't any such machine! There couldn't be such a machine! It's a lie and delirium! Why are you lying to us?"

In exhaustion Kavalerov dropped onto the chair.

"Listen, Kavalerov. Order yourself some beer and I'll tell you a tale. Listen."

TALE OF THE MEETING OF TWO BROTHERS

...Scaffolds surrounded the delicate, growing framework of 'Two Bits'.

Scaffolds are scaffolds: girders, tiers, ladders, passages, crossings, awnings—but various were the characters and eyes in the crowd gathering at the base. People smiled with diverse similarity. Some were inclined to simplicity and said: the structure is cross-hatched. Someone remarked:

"Wooden structures aren't supposed to grow too tall. The eye doesn't respect highly raised loads. The scaffolds reduce the grandeur of the structure. The tallest mast seems easily subject to destruction. Such an enormity of wood is delicate despite anything. The thought of fire suggests itself right away."

Another exclaimed:

"But on the other hand—look!—the beams were stretched out

like strings. A guitar, just exactly a guitar!"

To which the former remarked:

"Well now, I was talking about the delicacy of wood. Its lot is to serve music."

Then someone's mocking voice butted in:

"And brass? I, for instance, recognize only wind instruments."

A schoolboy found in the disposition of the boards an arithmetic noticed by no one, but to determine to what the crosses of multiplication signs referred and to where the equal signs led he didn't have time: the resemblance instantly disappeared, it was precarious.

"The Siege of Troy," thought a poet. "Siege towers."

And the comparison was confirmed by the appearance of musicians. Shielding themselves with horns they crawled into some sort of wooden trench toward the base of the structure.

Black was the evening, white and spherical the lanterns, the bunting showed unusually red, the gaps beneath the wooden slips were deathly black. The lanterns swung clanging their wires. As if the shadow was fluttering its eyebrows. Around the lanterns gnats flew and perished. From far off, forcing the windows along the way to blink, the contours of the surrounding houses, torn away by the lanterns, were carried and dashed against the structure—and then (until the lantern swung by the wind came to rest) the woods violently enlivened, everything came into motion—and, like a many-tiered sailing ship, the structure floated onto the crowd.

Along wood and onto wood toward the base of the structure passed Andrei Babichev. A tribunal constructed itself there. The orator received a stairway, and a stage and a rail and a blinding, black background and directly on himself—light. So much light was given that even distant observers saw the level of the water in the decanter on the table of the presidium.

Babichev moved above the crowd, very colorful and brilliant, sort of tiny, resembling an electric figurine. He was supposed to make a speech. Below, in the naturally formed shelter, actors were preparing for their performance. An oboe, invisible and incomprehensible to the crowd, howled sweetly. And incomprehensible, becoming silver, was the disk of the drum turned with its face toward the crowd. The actors were adorning themselves in the wooden gorge. Every step of a passer-by above moved the boards over them and disseminated sawdust in a fog.

The appearance of Babichev on the tribunal cheered up the public. They took him for the master of ceremonies. He was too fresh, deliberate, theatrical in appearance.

"Fatty! That's a real fatty!" one in the crowd got carried away.

"Bravo!" they yelled in various places.

But—"The floor is given to Comrade Babichev," they said from the presidium; and there was no trace of visibility left. Many rose up on their toes. Attention intensified. And it became pleasant for everyone. It was pleasant to see Babichev for two reasons: first—he was a well-known person, and second—he was fat. The fatness made the famous man one of them. They gave Babichev an ovation. Half of the applause welcomed his fatness. He made a speech.

He spoke about what the activities of 'Two Bits' would be: so many and so many dinners, such and such a capacity, such and such a percentage of nutritiousness and the kinds of advantages of communal feeding.

He spoke about the feeding of children: in 'Two Bits' there would be a children's section—about the scientific preparation of milk porridge, about the growth of children, about the backbone, about anemia. Like every orator he looked into the distance over the forward mass of spectators and therefore up to the very end of his speech remained indifferent to that which was going on below near the tribunal. And in the meantime some man in a derby had already long ago disturbed the attention of the forward spectators—those were no longer listening to the orator, being totally occupied by the man's behavior which, by the way, was perfectly peaceful. True, having separated from the crowd he did venture to get over the rope guarding the approaches to the tribunal; true, he was standing apart, which obviously showed some of his rights as either really belonging to him or as simply seized by him.... He—with his back to the public—stood leaning on the rope, or rather half sat on the rope hanging his rear over it, and not caring about what complete disorder would occur if the rope broke, imperturbably, apparently amused, swung himself on the rope.

Perhaps he was listening to the orator, or it's possible he was observing the actors. The dress of a ballerina flashed behind the

[91]

crossbeams, various funny faces peeped out in the little wooden window.

And.... Yes! What was really the most important thing? Well he, this somewhat eccentric man, came with a pillow. He carried in a yellow pillow case a large, old pillow slept on by many heads and, having settled on the rope, he lowered the pillow onto the ground—and the pillow sat down alongside like a pig.

And when the orator had finished his speech and, wiping his lips with a handkerchief, was pouring water out of the decanter with the other hand, when the applause was dying down and the public was switching its attention, preparing to listen to and watch the actors—the man with the pillow, raising his rear from the rope, got up to his full little height, stretched out the arm with the pillow and began shouting loudly:

"Comrades! I request the floor!"

The orator saw his brother Ivan. His fists clenched. Brother Ivan began rising along the stairs onto the tribunal. He ascended slowly. A man from the presidium ran up to the barrier. He was supposed to stop the stranger with gestures and voice, but his arm hung in the air and, as if counting the steps of the stranger along the stairs, his arm lowered in jerks.

"One... two... five... six."

"This is hypnosis!" They screeched in the crowd.

But the unknown walked, carrying the pillow by the scruff of its neck. A remarkable electrical figurine appeared on the black background. The background showed black as slate. The background was so black that there even seemed to be chalk lines on it, there was flickering in the eyes. The figurine stopped.

"A pillow!" passed through the crowd in a whisper.

And the stranger began to speak:

"Comrades! They want to take away your principal property from you: your home. The stallions of revolution, thundering along the back stairs, crushing our children and cats, breaking the tiles and bricks chosen by us, will burst into our kitchens. Women, under threat is your pride and glory—the home. They want to crush your kitchen with the elephants of revolution, mothers and wives!

"...What was he saying? He was scoffing at your pans, at little pots, at your quiet, at your right to stick a pacifier into your child's lips.... What is he teaching you to forget? What does he want to chuck out of your heart? Native home—home, sweet home! He wants

to make you tramps on the wild fields of history. Wives, he's spitting
into your soup. Mothers, he'd dreaming of erasing from the little
faces of your babes their resemblance to you—the sacred, beautiful,
family resemblance. He's bursting into your nooks, darts like a rat
along the shelves, into the hair of your armpits. Drive him to the
devil!... Here's a pillow. I'm the king of pillows. Tell him: we want to
sleep each on his own pillow. Don't touch our pillows! Our not-yet
fully-fledged heads red with chicken down have lain on these pillows,
our kisses have fallen on them in nights of love, we've died on them—
and those whom we've killed have died on them. Don't touch our
pillows! Don't call us! Don't beckon us, don't tempt us. What can
you offer us in place of our ability to love, to hate, to hope, to cry,
to pity and to forgive?.... Here's a pillow. Out coat of arms. Our stan-
dard. Here's a pillow. With a pillow we'll smother you..."

His speech broke off. But even so he'd said too much. It was as
though they'd grabbed him by the last sentence, as one might grab an
arm—they twisted his sentence behind his back. He stopped short,
suddenly becoming frightened, and the cause for fright was just that
the one against whom he was fulminating was standing silently, was
listening. And indeed the whole scene could have been taken for a
performance. Many even took it that way. After all, actors often appeared out of the audience. And what's more the real actors were
pouring out of the wooden shed. Yes, like nothing other than a butterfly the ballerina fluttered out from behind the boards. A clown in
a monkey suit crawled onto the tribunal, clutching at the crossbeams
with one hand and holding in the other a musical instrument of strange
appearance—a long, long horn with three bellmouths; and since one
might expect anything from a man in a monkey suit and a red wig,
the impression was easily given that he was crawling by some magi-
cal means along this very horn. Someone in a tail coat rushed about
under the tribunal catching the scattering actors, but these were
striving to catch sight of the extraordinary orator. Why even the actors too supposed that someone of the variety performers invited to
take part in the concert had thought up a stunt, come with a pillow,
entered into an argument with the speaker and would right way begin his usual act. But no. The clown slid down his idiotic horn in
fear. And the anxiety began. But the words thrown luxuriantly into
the crowd by the stranger did not sow the agitation. On the contrary,
the man's speech was taken as deliberate, exactly as a variety stunt;
rather the ensuing silence stirred the hair under many caps.

"Why are you looking at me?" asked the man, dropping the pillow.

The voice of a giant (no one knew that brother was speaking with brother), the whole square, the windows, the entrances heard the giant's short cry, old men raised themselves on their beds.

"Against whom are you waging war, scoundrel?" asked the giant.

His face bulged. It seemed there would leak out of this face, like out of a wine skin, from all over—from the nostrils, lips, ears— out of the eyes would come some sort of dark liquid and everyone would cover their eyes in horror.... He didn't say this. The boards around him, the cement, the clamps, the lines, the formulae finding flesh said this. It was their anger which was bursting him open.

But brother Ivan did not step back (everyone even expected: stepping back and stepping back, he would sit down on his pillow) on the contrary: suddenly he got stronger, straightened up, went up to the barrier, arranged his palm in a salute over his eyes and called:

"Where are you? I'm waiting for you! Ophelia!"

The wind swooped down. Gusts, however, were recurring all the time, the lanterns swayed. Those present had already become accustomed to the formation and disintegration of the figures of shadow (of squares, of Pythagorean pants, of little Hippocratic moons)—the many-tiered galleon of the structure continually broke loose from its anchor and sailed onto the crowd—so that a new gust turning many by the shoulder, bending many heads, would have been met with usual displeasure and immediately forgotten, if it weren't.... And it was said later: it blew past over heads, it flew up from behind.

Onto the crowd sailed the gigantic sailing ship, creaking with its wood, wailing with the wind, and a flying black body—like a bird against the rigging—hit against the high beam, plummeted, breaking a lantern....

"Are you scared, brother?" asked Ivan. "Here's what I'll do. I'll send her against the scaffolding. She'll destroy your erection. The screws will unscrew by themselves. The nuts will fall off, the con- crete will corrode like a leprous body. Well? She'll teach every beam how not to hold you. Well? Everything will collapse. She'll turn your every figure into a useless flower. There, brother Andrei, is what I can do...."

"Ivan, you're seriously ill. You're delirious, Ivan," suddenly softly and sincerely said the one from whom they expected threats.

"About whom are you talking? Who is this 'she?' I don't see anything. Who'll turn my figures into flowers? It was just the wind that knocked a lantern against a beam, the lantern just broke. Ivan, Ivan...."

And the brother stepped toward Ivan stretching out his arms. But that one pushed him aside.

"Look!" he exclaimed raising his hand. "No, you're not looking there.... That's it... more to the left.... Do you see? What's that sitting there on the girder? Do you see? Drink some water. Pour Comrade Babichev some water.... What's that seated there on the little pole? Do you see?!! Do you believe?!! Are you afraid?!!"

"That's a shadow!" said Andrei. "Brother, that's just a shadow. Let's get out of here. I'll give you a lift. Let the concert begin. The actors are tired. The public is waiting. Let's go, Vanya, let's go."

"Oh, a shadow? It's not a shadow, Andrusha. It's the machine which you laughed at.... It's me sitting on the little pole, me, the old world, my age sitting there. The brain of my age, Andrusha, capable of composing both songs and formulae. A brain full of the dreams which you want to destroy."

Ivan raised his hand and shouted:

"Go, Ophelia! I send you!"

And that which had sat down on the beam, flashing and turning, turned, began to rap, stamping as a bird raps and began to disappear in the dark gap between the crossings.

There was a panic, a crush, people ran howling. But it clattered making its way along the boards. Suddenly it emerged again emitting a ray of orange light, whistled—illusive in form—and as a weighty shadow gossamerically leaped higher perpendicularly into the chaos of boards, again took a seat on some edge, looked around....

"Operate, Ophelia! Operate!" shouted Ivan rushing along the tribunal. "Did you hear what he said about the home? I order you to destroy the erection...."

People ran and their running was accompanied by the running of the clouds, by the storm figure of the sky.

'Two Bits' collapsed....

The storyteller fell silent....

...The drum lay flat amidst the ruins and onto the drum scrambled I, Ivan Babichev. Ophelia hurried toward me, dragging the crushed and dying Andrei.

"Put me onto the pillow, brother," he whispered. "I want to die on the pillow. I give in, Ivan...."

I placed the pillow on my knees, he pressed his head to it.

"We've won, Ophelia," I said.

VII

In the morning on Sunday Ivan Babichev visited Kavalerov.

"Today I want to show you Valya," he announced solemnly.

They set out. One could call the walk charming. It was made through a deserted, festive city. They went in a roundabout way to Theater Square. There was almost no traffic. The slope along Tverskaya blued. Sunday morning—one of the best aspects of a Moscow summer. The illumination, not shattered by traffic, remained whole, as if the sun had just risen. Thus they walked along the geometrical maps of light and shadow, more likely: through stereoscopic bodies, because the light and shadow crossed not only along the flat surfaces but in the air as well. Not yet reaching the Mossoviet, they found themselves in full shadow. But into the space between two buildings fell a large massif of light. It was thick, almost dense; here it was already impossible to doubt that light is material: dust carried in it could have been taken for the vibration of the ether.

And here's the side street connecting Tverskaya with Nikitskaya. They stood awhile admiring a flowering hedge.

They entered the gate and ascended a wooden staircase to a glassed-in gallery, neglected but gay due to the abundance of panes of glass and the view of the sky through the lattice of these panes of glass.

The sky broke into plates of various blue color and nearness to the viewer. A fourth of all the panes of glass was knocked out. Into the lower row of little windows crawled the green tails of some plant crawling on the outside along the side of the gallery. Here everything was intended for a happy childhood. In such galleries rabbits are raised.

Ivan headed toward a door. There were three doors in the gallery. He walked toward the last.

On the way Kavalerov wanted to tear off one of the little green tails. He had hardly tugged when the whole system, invisible behind the side, stretched out after the little tail, and somewhere groaned some sort of wire, having meddled in the life of this ivy or devil knows what. (As if not in Moscow, but in Italy....) Making an effort Kavalerov pressed his temple against the window and saw the courtyard fenced off by a stone wall. The gallery was located at a height between the second and third floors. From such a height a view beyond the wall (Italy continued) onto a terribly green field was opened to him.

Yet entering onto the porch he heard voices and laughter. They carried from that field. He didn't manage to make out anything; Ivan distracted him. He knocked on the door. One, two, once again....

"No one's there," he mumbled. "She's already there...."

Kavalerov's attention remained on the glass knocked out over the lawn. Why? After all, as yet, nothing surprising had happened before his eyes. He caught only one step of some sort of motley movement, one stroke of the gymnastic rhythm of Ivan turning on the knock. Simply pleasant, sweet and cold was the green of the lawn for the vision, unexpected after the usual courtyard. In all probability, only later did he convince himself that the charm of the lawn had captured him so strongly right off.

"She's already left!" repeats Babichev. "Just permit me...."

And he looked into one of the little windows. Kavalerov lost no time in doing the same.

That which had produced on him the impression of a lawn turned out to be a small yard overgrown with grass. The main force of the green proceeded from the high, thickly-crowned trees standing along its sides. All of this greenery bloomed beneath the gigantic, blank wall of the building. Kavalerov was an observer from above. The whole neighborhood stretching out beyond the high point of observation loomed up over the yard. It lay like a doormat in a room full of furniture. Other people's roofs opened their secrets to Kavalerov. He saw a weather vane in natural size, little dormer windows of which no one below even suspects, and the forever irretrievable child's ball, which flew up too high once and rolled under the gutter. Structures studded with antennas went out by steps from the yard. The cupola of a church newly decorated with minium fell into an empty span of sky and, it seemed, flew until Kavalerov caught it with his glance. He saw the rocking shaft of a trolley mast from a far-off street and some other observer, leaning out of a faraway window and sniffing or eating something, submitting to the perspective, almost leaned on that rocking shaft.

And the main thing was the little yard.

They went downstairs. In the stone wall separating the courtyard from the little yard there was a flaw. A few stones were missing like loaves of bread taken out of an oven. In this embrasure they saw everything. The sun burned Kavalerov's crown. They saw jumping exercises. A rope was stretched between two poles. Having flown up, a boy carried his body over the rope sideways, almost gliding, stretching out parallel to the obstacle—as if he wasn't jumping but rolling over the obstacle like over an embankment. And rolling, he threw up his legs and pushed with them, similar to a swimmer repelling water. In the next fraction of a second his overturned, distorted face flashed, flying downward, and on the spot Kavalerov saw him standing on the ground; having hit the ground he emitted a sound similar to "aff" —half a cutoff exhalation, half the striking of heels against the grass.

Ivan tweaked Kavalerov on the elbow.

"There she is... look...." (In a whisper.)

Everyone began to shout and clap. The jumper, almost naked, moved off to the side, slightly limping on one foot, probably out of sportsman's coquetry.

This was Volodya Makarov.

Kavalerov was embarrassed. The feeling of shame and fear seized him. Smiling, Volodya displayed a whole sparkling mechanism of teeth.

Above, on the gallery, there was a knock on the door again. Kavalerov turned around. It was very stupid to be caught here by the wall peeping. Someone goes along the gallery. The little windows dismember the one walking. The parts of the body move independently. An optical illusion occurs. The head outstrips the trunk. Kavalerov recognizes the head. Along the gallery floats Andrei Babichev.

"Andrei Petrovich!" shouts Valya on the lawn. "Andrei Petrovich! Here! Here!"

The terrible guest disappeared. He abandons the gallery, looks for the way to the lawn. Various obstacles hide him from Kavalerov's eyes. It's necessary to escape.

"Here! Here!" rings Valya's voice.

Kavalerov sees: Valya is standing on the lawn having planted her feet apart widely and firmly. On her are black, highly tucked up shorts, her legs extremely bared, the whole structure of the legs in view. She's in white tennis shoes worn on bare feet; and the fact that the shoes are flat-soled makes her build still firmer and tighter—not feminine but masculine or puerile. Her legs are soiled, tanned, shiny. These are the legs of a little girl which are so often affected by the air, the sun, falls on tussocks, on the grass, blows, that they become coarse, get covered with wax-like scars from prematurely torn off scabs on scratches and their knees made rough like oranges. Age and subconscious confidence in her own physical resources give the possessor the right to hold her legs so carelessly, not to spare and not to cherish them. But higher, under the black shorts, the purity and tenderness of the body shows how beautiful the possessor will be, maturing and turning into a woman, when she herself will pay attention to herself and will want to adorn herself—when the scratches will heal, all the scabs will fall off, the tan will even out and turn into color.

He shook himself and ran along the blank wall in the opposite direction from the embrasure, smudging his shoulder against the stone.

"Where are you going!" Ivan called him. "Where are you running off to, wait!"

"He's shouting loudly! They'll hear!" Kavalerov became horrified. "They'll see me!"

Indeed, behind the wall it became distinctly quiet. They were listening there. Ivan caught up with Kavalerov.

"Listen, my dear.... Did you see? That's my brother! Did you see? Volodya, Valya.... All of them! the whole camp.... Wait, I'll crawl up onto the wall and curse them... you got smudged, Kavalerov, like a miller?"

Kavalerov said quietly:

"I know your brother perfectly well. It's he who chased me out. He—that important person about whom I told you.... Our fate is similar. You said that I had to kill your brother.... What am I to do?...

Valya sat on the stone wall.

"Dad!" she shrieked gasping.

Ivan clasped her legs hanging down from the wall.

"Valya, pluck out my eyes. I want to be blind," he said breathlessly, "I don't want to see anything: neither lawns, nor boughs, nor flowers, nor knights, nor coward—I have to become blind, Valya. I was mistaken, Valya.... I thought that all feelings had perished—love and devotion and tenderness.... But everything's remained, Valya.... Only not for us, and for us remained only envy and envy.... Pluck out my eyes, Valya, I want to become blind."

He slid along the girl's sweaty legs with his hands, face, chest and fell heavily toward the foot of the wall.

"Let's drink, Kavalerov," said Ivan. "We'll drink, Kavalerov, to youth, which has passed, to the conspiracy of feelings, which has collapsed, to the machine, which is not and will not be...."

"You're a son of a bitch, Ivan Petrovich! (Kavalerov grabbed Ivan by the collar.) Youth hasn't passed! No! Do you hear? It's not true! I'll prove it to you.... Tomorrow do you hear?—tomorrow at the soccer match I'll kill your brother...."

VIII

Nikolai Kavalerov took a place in the stands. Up above, to the right from him, in a wooden box, among the banners, the gigantic type of the posters, the ladders and cross boards sat Valya. Young people filled the box.

The wind blew; the day was very bright, transparent, whistled through by the wind from all sides. The enormous field showed green with flattened grass, shining like lacquer.

Without lowering his eyes, Kavalerov looked at the box, strained his vision and getting tired worked with his imagination, trying to obtain that which he could not see or hear from a distance. Not only he—many of those sitting next to the box, despite the fact that they were excited by anticipation of the exceptional spectacle, paid attention to the charming girl in the pink dress, almost a little girl, careless in a childish way of her poses and movements and at the same time having such a look that everyone wanted to be noticed by her, just as if she were a celebrity or the daughter of a celebrated person.

Twenty thousand spectators overcrowded the stadium. An unprecedented holiday was in progress—the long-awaited match between the Moscow and German teams.

In the stands people argued, shouted, brawled over nothing. An enormous number of people packed the stadium. Somewhere a railing broke with a duck cry. Kavalerov, getting tangled in the knees of others, in search of his place, saw how on the path at the foot of the stands, breathing heavily and arms outflung, lay a respectable old man in a cream-colored vest. They moved past him thinking little about him. The anxiety was strengthened by the wind. On the tower the flags beat like lightning.

Kavalerov's whole being strained toward the box. Valya was located above him, at an oblique, at about twenty meters. His vision taunted him. To him it seemed: their eyes met. Then he raised himself. To him it seemed: a medallion is flashing on her. The wind did with her what it wanted. She continually grabbed her hat. This was a hood of shining red straw. The wind blew her sleeve up to the very shoulder uncovering her arm, slender like a flute. A handbill flew away from her and, having flopped its wing, fell into a thicket.

Yet a month before the match it was conjectured that with the German team would come the famous Getzke playing center forward, that is, the main player of the five offense men. Indeed, Getzke arrived. As soon as the German team had come out onto the field to the sound of a march, and the players had not yet managed to place themselves along the field, the public (as it always happens) recognized the celebrity, although the celebrity was walking in the crowd of other guests.

"Getzke! Getzke!" the spectators began to shout, experiencing a peculiar gratification from the sight of the celebrated player and from the fact that they were clapping for him.

Getzke, who turned out to be a short, swarthy and round-shouldered man, stepped a little to the side, stopped, raised his hands over his head and brandished his joined palms. The unknown, foreign means of welcoming inspired the spectators still more.

The group of Germans—eleven persons—shone on the green in the purity of the air with the bright, oily coloring of their clothes. On them were orange, almost gold jerseys with greenish-lilac stripes on the right side of the chest and black shorts. The shorts fluttered in the wind.

Volodya Makarov, shivering a little from the freshness of the just-donned soccer shirt, was looking out of the soccer players' quarters through a window. The Germans reached the middle of the field.

"Let's go, eh?" he asked. "Let's go?"

"Let's go!" commanded the captain of the team.

The Soviet team ran out in red shirts and white shorts. The spectators fell onto the railings, thrashed with their feet against the boards.

The roar drowned out the music.

It fell to the Germans to play the first half of the game with the wind.

Ours not only played and tried to do everything which is supposed to be done in order to play as well as possible but in addition did not cease to observe the Germans' game as professionals. The game continues for ninety minutes with a short break after forty-five minutes. After the break the teams change halves of the field. So that in windy weather it's more advantageous to play against the wind with fresh strength.

Since the Germans were playing with the wind, and the wind was very strong, the whole game was blown toward our goal. The ball almost never left the Soviet half of the field. Our backs gave strong "sparks," that is, high, parabolic kicks, but the ball, sliding along the wall of the wind, turned, sparkling with yellow, and rambled backwards. The Germans attacked fiercely. The celebrated Getzke turned out to be really and truly a formidable player. All attention focused on him.

When the ball fell to him, Valya, sitting on high, screeched as if at once, immediately, she was bound to see something horrible and criminal. Getzke was bursting toward the goal. Then Valya, swinging toward her neighbor, grabbed her neighbor's arm with both hands, pressed her cheek to it and, thinking only of one thing, to hide her face and not see the horrible, continued to watch with squinted eyes the frightful movements of Getzke, black from running in the heat.

But Volodya Makarov, goalkeeper of the Soviet team, caught the ball. Getzke, not yet having completed the movement made for the kick, gracefully changed this movement for another needed in order to turn and run, turned and ran, bending his back tightly covered with the jersey sweat-soaked to blackness. Instantly Valya assumed a natural pose and began to laugh: first, with delight that they didn't drive the ball in on our side, and second—because she remembered how recently she was squealing and grabbing her neighbor's arm.

"Makarov! Makarov! Bravo, Makarov!" she shouted with everyone.

Every minute the ball flew at the goal. It struck against its bars, they moaned, lime fell off them. Volodya grabbed the ball in a sort of flight, when this seemed mathematically impossible. The whole audience, the whole living slope of the stands became as if sheerer— each spectator rose, shoved by the frightful, impatient desire to see at last the most interesting—the score of the goal. The referee threw the whistle into his lips on the run, prepared to whistle the score. Volodya did not catch the ball—he plucked it from the line of flight and, as if violating physics, subjected himself to the stunning effect of indignant forces. He flew up together with the ball, whirling, literally getting screwed on to it: he clasped the ball with his whole body—knees, stomach and chin, throwing his weight onto the velocity of the ball, as they throw rags to put out a flare-up. The intercepted velocity of the ball threw Volodya sidewards two meters; he fell in the form of a colored paper bomb. The enemy forwards ran toward him, but in the end the ball turned up high above the battle.

Volodya remained in the goal. He couldn't stand still. He walked along the line of the goal from one pole to the other, surpressing the gust of energy called forth by the struggle with the ball. Everything buzzed in him. He moved his arms, shook himself, tossed up lumps of earth with his toe. Trim before the beginning of the game, now he consisted of rags, a black body and the leather of the enormous finger-less gloves. The respites didn't continue for long. Once again the attack of the Germans rolled to the Moscow goal. Volodya desired victory for his side with a passion and worried about each of his players. He thought that he only knew how one has to play against Getzke, what his weak sides are, how to defend against his attack. It interested him too, what sort of opinion had formed in the famous German of the Soviet game. When he himself applauded and shouted "hurrah" to each of his backs, he felt right then like shouting to Getzke:

"That's how we play! Do we play well in your opinion?"

As a soccer player Volodya represented a complete opposite to Getzke. Volodya was a professional sportsman—the other was a professional player. Important to Volodya was the general course of the game, the overall victory, the outcome—Getzke strove only to show his own skill. He was an old, experienced player, not intending to maintain the honor of the team: he valued only his own success; he was not a permanent member of any sort of sports organization be-cause he had compromised himself by moves from club to club for money. They forbade him to participate in matches for the play-off of a championship. They invited him only for friendly games, demon-stration matches and trips to other countries. Skill united in him with luck. His participation made the team dangerous. He was suspicious of the players—both those with whom he played and the opponents. He knew that he would drive in the balls on any team. The rest was not important to him. He was a hack.

As early as the middle of the game it became clear to the spec-tators that the Soviet team was not yielding to the Germans. They were conducting the correct attack—Getzke was hindering this. He spoiled, destroyed their combinations. He was playing only for himself at his own risk without help and without helping. Receiving the ball, he drew all the movement of the game to himself, squeezed it into a lump, loosened and sloped it, transferred it from one edge to another—according to his own plans, obscure to his partners, relying only on himself, on his running and abilities to dodge the opponent.

Hence the spectators concluded that the second half of the game, when Getzke would rest and when our boys would receive the windy side, would end with the rout of the Germans. If only right now our boys could hold out, not letting even one ball through into their goal.

But this time, too, the virtuoso Getzke achieved his own. Ten minutes before the break he burst toward the right edge, carried the ball with his body, then stopped sharply, cutting off the pursuers, who, not expecting the stop, ran out ahead and to the right, turned with the ball toward the center, and through an open space, dodging only one Soviet back, drove the ball straight toward the goal, frequently glancing now at his feet, now at the goal, as if proportioning and calculating the velocity, directions, and timing of the kick.

A continuous "o-o-o" in a howl rolled from the stands.

Volodya, bowing his legs and placing his arms as if he were holding an invisible barrel, prepared to catch the ball. Getzke, not kicking, ran up to the goal. Volodya fell under his legs. The ball became hidden between the two of them as in a barrel; then the whistles and tramping of the spectators covered the finale of the scene. From a kick of one of the two the ball lightly and unevenly flew up over the head of Getzke, and he pounded it into the net with a jerk of his head similar to a bow.

Thus a goal was scored against the Soviet team.

The stadium roared. Binoculars turned in the direction of the Soviet goal. Getzke, looking at his gleaming shoes, coquettishly ran to the center.

Comrades picked up Volodya.

IX

Valya turned together with everyone else. Kavalerov saw her

face turned toward him. He didn't doubt that she saw him. He started
to fuss: a strange supposition made him angry. It appeared to him that
those around were laughing—they had noticed his anxiety.

He looked around at those sitting alongside. And it was very
unexpected that in one corner with him, in the near vicinity, sat
Andrei Babichev. Once again Kavalerov was revolted by the two
white hands regulating the hinge of the binoculars, the massive trunk
in the gray jacket, the trimmed moustache....

Like a black projective the binoculars hung over Kavalerov.
The straps of the binoculars hung down like reins from Babichev's
cheeks.

The Germans were already advancing again.

Suddenly the ball, thrown out by someone's powerful and un-
calculated kick, flew up high and sideways beyond the field, out of
the game, in the direction of Kavalerov, whistled over the ducked
heads of the lower rows, stopped for an instant and, all its laminae
twirling, crashed down into the boards, towards Kavalerov's feet. The
game stopped. The players froze, overcome by surprise. The picture
of the field, green and variegated, moving all the time, now all of a
sudden turned to stone. Thus a motion picture stops all of a sudden
at the moment of a break in the film, when they are already turning
the light on in the theater but the projectionist has not yet managed
to turn out the light, and the audience sees the strangely whitening
still and the contours of the hero, absolutely motionless in that pose,
which speaks of vast rapid movement. Kavalerov's anger intensified.
Everyone around laughed. A ball falling in the seats always evokes
laughter: as if at that minute the spectators realize the true comical-
ness of the fact that for half an hour people have been running after
a ball, inducing them—the spectators, the bystanders—to accept their
completely frivolous pastime with such seriousness and passion.

All of the thousands at this minute, as much as they were able,
presented Kavalerov their unsolicited attention, and this attention
was laughable.

It's possible that Valya, too, was laughing at him, the person
caught under the ball! It's possible that she's enjoying herself doubly,
jeering at an enemy in a funny situation. He smirked, moving his
foot aside from the ball which, losing support, with catlike affection

again bumped against his heel.

"Well!" involuntarily and amazedly shouted Babichev.

Kavalerov was passive. Two big white palms reached out for the ball. Someone picked up the ball and passed it to Babichev. He stood up to his full height and, sticking out his stomach, tilted his arms in order to throw farther. He couldn't be serious in such a thing and understanding that it's necessary to be serious, exaggerated the outward expression of seriousness, frowning and pouting his fresh, red lips.

Babichev, heavily swaying forward, hurled the ball, magically unfettering the field.

"He doesn't recognize me," Kavalerov harbored his anger.

The first half of the game ended with the score "one to nothing" in favor of the German team.... The players, with dark streaks on their faces, covered with threads of grass, went toward the passage moving their naked knees heavily and widely as in water. The Germans, outlandishly red, with a blush beginning at the temples, mixed gaily with the Muscovites. The players walked seeing everyone at once, the whole crowd under the boarded wall of the passage, and seeing no one individually. They smeared over the crowd with smiles and lifeless eyes, too transparent on their darkening faces. The people to whom they had just seemed like little, running and falling, multicolored figurines, now met them close up. The not yet cooling noise of the game moved together with them. Getzke, resembling a gypsy, watched, sucking a little wound just received above the elbow.

To the idlers the novelty was the details of the height or build of this or that player, the severity of the scratches, the heavy breathing, the complete disarray of the clothing. From afar everything produced a lighter, more festive impression.

Kavalerov was squeezed between the sides of others under some sort of crossbeam and was relieved to get down onto the grass. Here, in the shade, he ran along the path with the others, skirting the stands from the back side. The refreshment stand, placed on the lawn under the trees, filled up in an instant. The rumpled little old man in the cream-colored vest, still discontentedly and cautiously looking at the public, was eating ice cream. A crowd clung to the soccer players' quarters.

"Hurrah! Makarov! Hurrah!" excited shouts carried from there. The fans clambered up onto the fences, defending themselves against the barbed wire as against bees—and higher: onto the trees, into the dark green, swaying from the wind and adroitness, like wood dwarfs.

Obliquely over the crowd a shiny body gushing with nakedness flew up. They were swinging Volodya Makarov.

Kavalerov lacked the spirit to pass beyond the triumphal ring. Hanging around behind the crowd he peeped through the cracks.

Volodya was already standing on the ground. The stocking on his one leg lowered, rolling up into a green bagel around his pear-shaped, slightly hairy calf. The mutilated shirt barely held on to his trunk. He chastely crossed his arms on his chest.

And here stands Valya. And Andrei Babichev is with her.

The idlers are applauding all three.

Babichev looks lovingly at Volodya.

The wind intervened. A striped peg fell; all the leaves swung to the right. The ring of idlers disintegrated, the whole picture fell apart, people were escaping the dust. Valya caught it more than anyone. The pink dress, light like husks, flew up over her legs, showing Kavalerov its transparence. The wind blew the dress against her face, and Kavalerov saw the contour of her face in the radiance and translucency of the fabric spreading like a fan. Kavalerov saw this through the dust, and how, catching her dress, she whirled, got tangled, nearly falling sideways. She tried to slam the hem down on her knees, to squeeze it, but she didn't manage it, and then, to terminate the indecency, she resorted to half measures: she clasped her overly exposed legs with her arms, hiding the knees, folding up double, like a bather taken unawares.

Somewhere the referee whistled. A march rolled off. Thus the gay confusion was interrupted. They were beginning the second half of the game. Volodya dashed.

"A minimum of two goals on the Germans!" screeched a boy rushing past Kavalerov.

Valya continued to struggle with the wind. In the chase after the hem she changed position ten times and in the end found herself close to Kavalerov, at the distance of a whisper.

She stood, legs planted widely apart. Her hat, thrown off by
the wind and caught in flight, she held in her hand. Not yet recovering from the jump she looked at Kavalerov without seeing him, tilting her head to the side a little with its short, chestnut hair cut sharply at the cheeks. The sunlight slid over her shoulder, she swayed and
her collar bones flashed like daggers. The viewing lasted a tenth of a
minute and growing cold, Kavalerov immediately understood what
an incurable yearning would remain in him forever because he had
seen her, a being of another world, alien and extraordinary, and
sensed how depressingly inaccessible her purity was—both because
she was a little girl and because she loved Volodya—and how unre-
solvable her seductiveness was.

Babichev was waiting for her, stretching out his arm.

"Valya," said Kavalerov. "I've been waiting for you my whole
life. Take pity on me...."

But she didn't hear. She ran, undercut by the wind.

X

That night Kavalerov returned home drunk.

He passed along the corridor toward the sink—to drink. He unturned the faucet as far as it would go; he got all soaked. He left the
faucet; the stream trumpeted. Entering Annechka's room he stopped.
The light was not put out. Blanketed with the yellow cotton of the
light, the widow sat on her enormous bed dangling her naked legs
over the side. She was ready for sleep.

Kavalerov took a step. She was silent as though spellbound. It
appeared to Kavalerov that she was smiling, enticing.

He went at her.

She did not resist and even opened an embrace.

"Oh you're a little creeper," she whispered, "hey you, little
creeper."

Later he was waking up. Thirst tormented him, the drunken,
frenzied dream of water. He was waking up—there was quiet. A sec-

ond before awakening he remembered how the stream was pounding into the sink—the sharp memory tossed him up but there was no water. He fell down again. While he slept the widow played the mistress: she shut the faucet, undressed the sleeper and repaired his suspenders. Morning arrived. At first Kavalerov didn't understand anything. Like a drunkard-beggar in a comedy, picked up by a rich man and brought into a palace, he lay, senseless, amidst unfamilar luxury. He saw his own unprecedented reflection in the mirror—feet forward. He lay magnificently, turning his arm up behind his head. The sun illuminated him from the side. Just as in the cupola of a temple he soared in wide, smoking strips of light. And above him bunches of grapes hung, cupids danced, apples rolled out of cornucopias—and he almost heard coming from all of this a solemn, organ hum. He lay on Annechka's bed.

"You remind me of him," Annechka whispered hotly leaning over him.

Over the bed hung a glass-covered portrait. Hanging was a man, someone's young grandfather, solemnly dressed—in one of the latest frock-coats of the period. One could feel: he had a firm, many-barreled nape. A man of about fifty-seven.

Kavalerov remembered: father is changing his shirt....

"You reminded me very much of my husband," Annechka repeats, embracing Kavalerov. And Kavalerov's head passes into her armpit as into a tent. The widow opened the tents of her armpits. Excitement and shame raged in her.

"He also took me... like that... by cunning... quietly, he was silent, so silent, didn't say anything... and then! Ah you're my little creeper..."

Kavalerov struck her.

She was dumbfounded. Kavalerov jumped from the bed, ploughup layers of linen; the sheets stretched out after him. She rushed toward the door, her arms howled for help, she ran, pursued by her belongings, like a Pompeian woman. A basket tumbled down; a chair listed.

He struck her several times across the back, in the waist girded with fat as with a tire.

The chair stood on one leg.

"He also beat me," she said smiling through tears.

Kavalerov returned to the bed. He collapsed, feeling that he was getting sick. He lay unconscious all day. In the evening the widow lay down beside. She snored. Kavalerov imagined her larynx in the form of an arch leading into darkness. He hid behind the vaults of the arch. Everything shook, trembled; the ground shook. Kavalerov slipped and fell under the pressure of the air fluttering out of the abyss. The sleeper whined. At once she stopped whining, fell silent, champing loudly. The whole architecture of the larynx became distorted. Her snore became powdery, seltzery.

Kavalerov tossed and cried. She got up and put a wet towel on his forehead. He reached for the moisture, raising his whole self up slightly, searched for the towel with his hands, bunched it up, putting it under his cheek and kissed it, whispering:

"They've stolen her. How difficult it is for me to live in the world.... How difficult...."

And the widow, not managing to lie down, fell asleep at once, sticking to the mirror arch. Sleep coated her with sweetness. She slept with an open mouth, gargling, as old women sleep.

Bedbugs abided, rustled, as if someone was ripping the wallpaper. The bedbugs' hiding places, unknown to the day, appeared. The tree of the bed grew, swelled.

The window-sill began to turn pink.

Dusk curled around the bed. Night secrets came down from the corners along the walls, flowed round the sleepers and crawled under the bed.

Kavalerov suddenly sat up, opening his eyes widely.

Over the bed stood Ivan.

XI

And immediately Kavalerov began to get ready.

Annechka was sleeping in a sitting position under the arch, roping off her stomach with her arms. Carefully, in order not to disturb her, he drew off the blanket and having put it on like a cloak, appeared in front of Ivan.

"Just perfect," said the latter. "You sparkle like a lizard. That's the way you'll present yourself to the people too. Come, come! We must hurry."

"I'm very sick" sighed Kavalerov; he smiled meekly, as if excusing himself for the fact that he din't have the desire to look for his pants, jacket and shoes. "It doesn't matter that I'm barefoot?"

Ivan was already in the corridor. Kavalerov hurried after him.

"I've suffered long and without reason," thought Kavalerov. "Today the day of atonement has arrived."

The flow of people grabbed them. Around the nearest corner opened a shining road.

"There it is!" said Ivan squeezing Kavalerov's hand. There's 'Two Bits!' "

Kavalerov saw: gardens, spherical cupolas of leafage, an arch of light, transparent stone, galleries, the flight of a ball over the greenery....

"Here!" commanded Ivan.

They ran along a wall crushed by ivy, then they had to jump. The blue blanket made the jump easier for Kavalerov; he floated through the air over the crowd and descended to the base of the widest stone staircase. Getting scared at once, he began to crawl under his blanket, like an insect folding its wings. They didn't notice him. He sat down behind a socle.

At the top of the staircase, surrounded by many people, stood Andrei Babichev. He stood with one arm around Volodya, squeezing him toward himself.

"They'll bring her right away," said Andrei smiling to friends.

And here Kavalerov saw the following: along the asphalt road leading to the steps of the staircase came an orchestra and above the orchestra soared Valya. The sounding of the instruments held her in the air. The sound carried her. Now she ascended, now descended over the trumpets, depending on the pitch and intensity of the sound. Her ribbons flew up higher than her head, her dress inflated, her hair stood up.

The final passage threw her onto the top of the staircase, and she fell into Volodya's arms. Everyone stepped aside. In the circle remained the two of them.

What followed Kavalerov didn't see. A sudden horror seized him. A strage darkness moved out in front of him. Turning to ice, he slowly turned around. On the grass behind him sat Ophelia.

"Ah-ah-ah!" he began to shout fearfully. He darted to escape. Tinkling, Ophelia grabbed him by the blanket. It slid off. In a shameful state, stumbling, falling, striking his jaw against the stone, he climbed up the staircase. The people looked on from above. Bending over stood the lovely Valya.

"Ophelia, back!" resounded Ivan's voice. "She's not listening to me... Ophelia, stop!"

"Hold her!"

"She'll kill him!"

"Oh!"

"Look! Look! Look!"

Kavalerov looked around from the middle of the staircase. Ivan was making attempts to scramble up onto the wall. The ivy broke. The crowd rushed back. Ivan hung on the wall on his widely spread arms. The horrible iron thing moved slowly along the grass in his direction. From that which one might have called the head of the thing a sparkling needle quietly moved out. Ivan howled. His hands didn't hold. He fell off; his derby rolled among the dandelions. He sat, pressing his back up against the wall, covering his face with his arms. The machine moved, picking dandelions along the way.

Kavalerov got up and in a voice full of despair began to shout:

"Save him! You're not really going to allow a machine to kill a man?!"

No answer followed.

"My place is with him!" said Kavalerov. "Teacher! I'll die with you."

But it was already late. Ivan's hare-like wail forced him to fall down. Falling, he saw Ivan pinned to the wall by the needle.

Ivan inclined gently, turning around on the horrible axis.

Kavalerov wrapped up his head in his arms so as not to see or hear anything more. But all the same he heard the clanging. The machine was ascending the staircase.

"It's not what I want!" he began to shout with all his might. "She'll kill me! Forgive me! Forgive me! Have mercy on me! It's not I who disgraced the machine. I'm not guilty. Valya! Valya! Save me!"

XII

Kavalerov was sick for three full days. Recovering, he escaped.

He got down, gazing at one spot in the corner under the bed. He got dressed like an automaton and suddenly felt a new leather loop on his suspenders. The widow has removed the safety pin. Where did she get the loop? Ripped it off of her husband's old suspenders? Kavalerov understood fully the loathsomeness of his position. He ran into the corridor without his jacket. On the way he unhooked and threw away the red suspenders.

On the threshold of the landing he lingered. No voices were heard from the courtyard. Then he stepped onto the landing, and all of his thoughts became confused. The sweetest sensations arose— languor, joy. The morning was lovely. There was a light breeze (as though a book were being leafed through), the sky shone blue. Kavalerov stood over a dirtied place. A cat, frightened by his fit, rushed out of a garbage can; some sort of trash poured down after it. What of the poetic could there be in this pigpen invested with so many curses? But he stood there, his head thrown back, stretching out his arms.

At that second he felt that now the time had arrived, that now the border between two existences had been drawn—the time of catastrophe. To break, to break with everything which was... right away, immediately, in two heart beats, no more—it's necessary to step over the border, and a life, repulsive, hideous, not his—an alien, forced life—would be left behind....

He stood, opening his eyes widely, and his whole field of vision, due to the run and the excitement and because he was still weak, pulsated before him and turned pink.

He understood the degree of his fall. It was supposed to pass.

He was living a too easy, self-sufficient life, he had too high an opinion of himself—he, lazy, unclean and lewd....

Flying over the pigpen Kavalerov understood everything.

He returned, picked up the suspenders, dressed. A spoon tinkled—the widow reached out for him—but without looking around he left the house. Once again he spent the night on the boulevard. And once again he returned. But he had decided firmly!

"I'll put the widow in her place. I won't allow her even to mention what happened. All kinds of things happen on a spree. But I can't live on the street."

The widow was lighting a splinter over the stove. She looked at him out from behind her temple and smiled complacently. He went into the room. Put onto the corner of the cupboard was Ivan's derby.

Ivan was sitting on the bed, looking like his brother, only a little smaller. The blanket surrounded him like a cloud. On the table stood a wine bottle. Ivan was gulping red wine from a glass. Apparently he had awakened recently; his face had still not evened out after sleep, and he was still scratching sleepily somewhere beneath the blanket.

"What does this mean?" Kavalerov asked the classic question.

Ivan smiled serenely.

"This means, my friend, that we must have a drink. Annechka, a glass."

Annechka entered. Got into the cupboard.

"Don't you be jealous, Kolya," she said embracing Kavalerov. "He's very lonely, the same sort as you. I feel sorry for you both."

"What does this mean?" Kavalerov asked quietly.

"Well why harp on it?" Ivan got angry. "It means nothing."

He got down from the bed, holding up his underwear, and poured Kavalerov some wine.

"Let's drink, Kavalerov.... We talked a lot about feelings.... And the main thing, my friend, we forgot.... About indifference... Isn't it true? Indeed... I think that indifference is the best of the states of the human mind. We'll be indifferent, Kavalerov. Look! We've found peace, my dear. Drink. To indifference. Hurrah! To Annechka! And today, by the way... listen: I'll.... inform you of something pleasant... today, Kavalerov, it's your turn to sleep with Annechka. Hurrah!"